Branch of the Everlong

Epic of Hornblood Castle #3

Eric Kercher

Paper and Sword, LLC

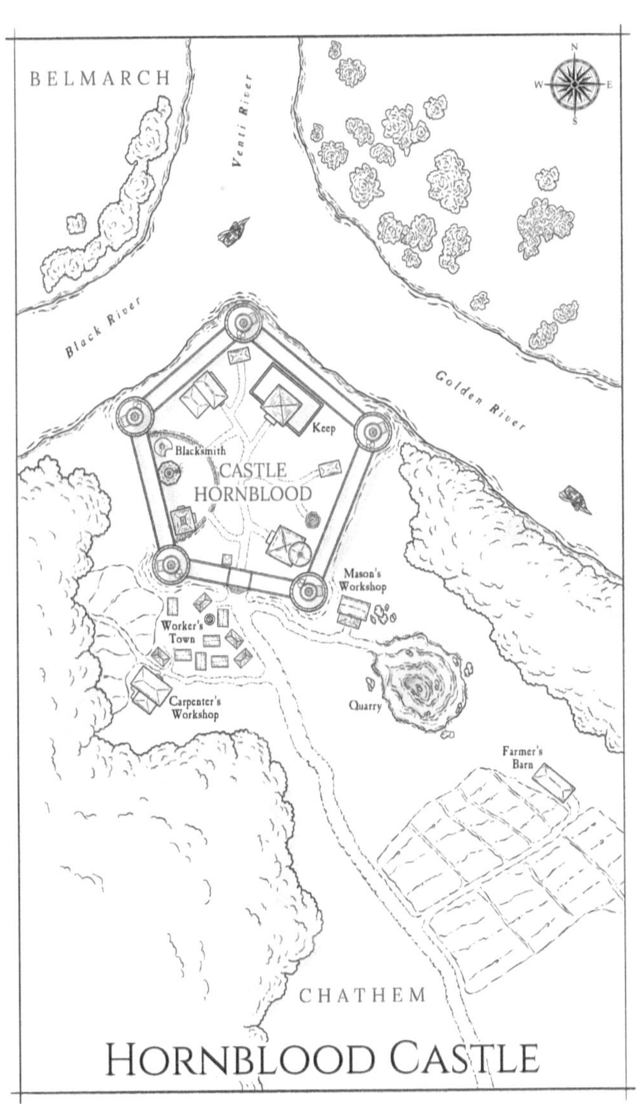

HORNBLOOD CASTLE

To Nina, a wonderful and loving mother who always believed
in me.

From the Author

There are days when we all need an escape from a terrible job, a terrible day, or a terrible life.

Join my newsletter and get an escape from the real world, stories, and lore designed to entertain and delight.

You'll also get *Stories from the Deep*, an exclusive, unpublished anthology chock full of extra epilogues, short stories, and lore from the Patmos Sea Fantasy Adventure Series.

Join now at erickercher.com.

Enjoy the book.

-Eric Kercher

1

Hunter for the Hunted

Scritch, scratch. Little legs pattered by in the darkness. Sam waited patiently, even though his mind was telling him to move.

Small squeaks echoed in the room, the dark hollows of the castle basement.

It was getting closer. It scuffed and shuffled. He smelled horrible, covered in refuse and his unwashed scent from weeks of the same clothes and no chance to get them clean.

Behind the creature water dripped in a slow, steady flow. His belly gnawed at his ribcage, almost on fire.

He had to wait.

It got closer, and then it was there. Sam lunged.

The rat tried to move, but his blade found it faster. Red, glowing eyes stared at him as it hissed and spat, trying to scratch him.

He was breathing hard, even though he hadn't moved more than a foot. This was a big one, and he was pleased.

The movements died, the screams of the rat slowing and then dying away.

Sam panted in the darkness. Warm blood covered his hand. He pulled his prey up and slung it over his shoulder.

Up the stairs he climbed, one foot in front of the other. Like every day he wondered whether Rhys had made it. Not knowing ate at him more than the hunger.

He stopped at the top of the stairs to catch his breath and slow his pounding heart, leaning against the cold, hard wall.

Sam put his head against it, letting the rough, cool stone suck the heat from his head, and coughed.

It was a dry, rasping cough. His leg throbbed, the old wounds coming back to him. When he had recovered enough, he opened the door.

Blinking against the light, Sam stepped out of the dungeons of the Keep and into the hall. He was still inside, but light trickled in from the rooms up ahead.

Voices drifted in, and he shuffled to them. He took a look at his blood-drenched hand, already drying off, and thought about washing.

He winced, thinking of the freezing cold water against his skin. That they still had plenty of, if they could break the ice off the top of the well.

"Sam!" Martha exclaimed, cutting off her conversation with Belinda. "What happened to you?"

"I've killed the thing eating our food." Sam dropped the rat on the counter. Its tongue rolled out of its mouth, but the rest of it was going stiff. "I know it isn't appetizing, but I thought we could eat it. I thought it fitting."

He slumped into a chair. So little strength, there was too little of it left in his body. He eyed the rat, thinking of how its flesh might taste.

Warm and succulent, roasted over a nice, crackling fire. Dripping with fat. Sam's mouth watered.

"I'll do what I can," Martha said.

Belinda was staring at him, a hint of a glare subdued by her exhaustion.

"Give it to the boy," Sam said. He was getting so thin it broke his heart every time he saw those little cheeks.

Beady little eyes poked out from the blanket at her chest. He moved, coughed, then started crying.

Belinda turned and comforted him, rocking him back and forth and shushing him. She shot him one last glare and walked out of the kitchen.

The rat wouldn't last. They would eat of all it, that he knew for sure, down to cracking the bones to get to the marrow. They needed the meat.

He felt a wave of sadness wash over him that this is what it had come to. Sam tried to control it, but he was so tired.

How long has it been since Rhys left in the boat? It was all a haze now, the fog that never left his brain seeping through his body.

Sam sniffed. He averted his gaze, aware that Belinda didn't take too kindly to him. His heart ached at that too, wished he could do something about it, but he knew that her sadness and grief overruled everything else. She had gone so long with hate in her that he wasn't sure it would ever go away.

And that ate at him too, gnawing worse than the hunger did.

He wanted to make it go away but knew that she was in total control of the situation.

"That is... kind of you," Martha said, snapping him out of his thoughts and back to reality.

"I hate to see him like that. He should be fat and happy, not sticks and bones poking through his skin." His own skin felt tight, as he suspected everyone else's did. Fat was in short supply within the walls of the castle.

"I'll see what I can do about cooking it." Martha stared at the dead rat. She pushed up her sleeves and took out a knife, sharpening it with quick, efficient strokes, only expending enough energy to get it sharp enough to slice underneath the matted fur and skin, parting it from the muscle with quick slices.

"I can bring you something to burn." There wasn't much left, but he could find scraps to use. A few sticks might do for a fire. His mouth watered just watching her cut the measly strips of meat from the tiny bones.

A few moments of work and the rat was dressed and ready to eat, organs and all. "I'll put it into a stew." Martha looked around and pulled out a small pot. "This will do."

Sam eased himself into the corner, sliding down the stone until he was supported by the floor. It was cold too, no way to escape it. The smell of the rat, blood and bone and meat, drifted over to him and tortured him. His breath was coming in short gasps. "Let me rest, and then I will go out to the workshop."

His eyelids felt heavy and tried to drift shut, but he didn't let them. After a few minutes, and while Martha prepared every-thing, his breathing steadied, and Sam got back to his feet. He nodded in her direction and walked out to the workshop, bracing himself for the cold before opening the Keep door and walking out into the snow and wind.

It wasn't as cold as it had been, but it was still brutal on his body. He was shivering within a few seconds, and his hands fumbled when he finally reached the workshop and pulled out the smallest scraps of wood he could. The wood pile was down to almost nothing. They had burned almost everything else and were scavenging beams from the castle when they had the strength at the beginning of the day.

He couldn't get Archie's face out of his mind as he worked, and the faces of all the others that had died. They walked in a long, sad line through his mind, just staring at him. It was enough, and he felt a mixture of shame and sadness as they did.

After that, and while he walked back to the Keep, came the worst of it. The children, emaciated and thin, still living, but only just, came to mind. He wanted to close his eyes when he got inside but didn't. A few of them peered out at him from the pile of bodies, watching him cross the room with curiosity until he slipped out of view and down the hall.

They were all counting on him to survive, and there was nothing he could do about it now. Their fate rested with Overseer Rhys and his luck, for better or for ill.

"This is all I could find that was handy," Sam said as he entered the kitchen. Martha looked at it with tired eyes and nodded. He got to work lighting the fire under the pot, a strange sight in a fireplace so large to be confined to such as small fire. They could have thrown in a quarter of the tree and burned it, and probably would in the future.

If they survived.

The fire caught, and smoke filled the kitchen. The tiny amount of heat coming from it was a blessing, and Martha pressed up beside him to share in it. Soon they had a small fire, and the pot pressed against it.

She was so close, and warm. *It feels nice, in a way.* That strange fluttering feeling came back in his stomach, pushing aside the hunger for a few blessed moments.

He knew he should say something, but he wasn't sure what. He was keenly aware of every part of her touching him. She moved, reaching out a hand to stir the pot with a long spoon. That side of his body was chilled, used to the warmth of her skin, wrapped up in all the clothing she could find.

Sam cleared his throat. "What do you think we will do in spring?"

Martha looked at him. A lock of her hair fell down over her eye. "What do you mean by that question?"

"I'm not sure." Sam looked away. "Trying to pass the time, I imagine."

"I pray that we make it to spring." He looked back at her, but she was staring at the fire. It was dancing, sending up small tufts of smoke that curled up the chimney. Sam wanted to reach down and hold it in his hand, bring it near to his bosom to suck up its warmth, but he restrained himself and savored the momentary feeling of warmth it gave him, little as it may be. "I'm afraid the food will be gone next week."

He knew it was coming, but it still hit him in the stomach like a punch to the gut. All their rationing and scrimping, all of it was for nothing. "It will run out when it runs out. We'll have to go on after that."

"Until when? When we die?" She had tears in the corner of her eyes. "The children..."

"If there was anything you could do for them you would have done it already." Martha bit her thumb and squeezed her eyes shut. She looked so vulnerable, so frail.

Sam wanted to reach out and take her hand, sweep her into his arms and hold her. For all her iron appearance, her harsh way with the other girls in the castle, this was another side that he had never seen.

A breeze from the window gusted through the kitchen and the fire sputtered dangerously. Sam reached out his hands to shield it. The pot hadn't boiled yet.

What am I supposed to say, what am I supposed to do? Sam chewed at his lip. Martha wiped her eyes.

"Here I am blubbering when there's a job to do." She stirred the pot again. "What must you think of me?"

"I think you care about everyone around you." Sam swallowed. "I... admire you for it."

Their eyes locked. Sam felt his face flush, steam rising to his cheeks. Martha was searching his eyes, looking for something, but he wasn't sure what. "The soup is ready."

His heart was pounding. He could still feel the heat from her body on him, but it was gone an instant later when she stood and took the pot from the fire. It had been boiling. For how long, he wasn't sure, but the fire was dying down and the wood had been almost all consumed.

"Did I say something wrong?" Sam stood too.

"Will you get Belinda for me?" Martha poured the soup into waiting bowls. She refused to make eye contact with him, but worked with a steady, practiced hand.

His mind was a rush of emotions and thoughts tripping over each other. What had he said to make her act this way? Was it him saying she cared about everyone? *I can't see why that would make her angry.*

All he could do was turn and leave, searching for Belinda and her child. He found her in the great hall, huddled up against the mass of bodies, and signaled for her.

The confusion was still in him, but there was also a strange sense of anger with it. It must have shown in his face, because Belinda looked at him with a soft expression of alarm and clutched her child closer. Still, she followed him into the hall, away from the others.

"What is it? What have I done?" she asked when they were out of earshot of the others, in a hissing whisper.

"You've done? Nothing you've done." Sam took a deep breath, calmed himself. "I'm sorry, it's just...you wouldn't understand."

"Hold on." Belinda had been following him, but at the words he turned to see her stopped. Gone was the expression of concern, now replaced with one of anger. "Have you hurt her?"

"Hurt who?" Sam took a step back and raised his hands. "Martha. Have you broken her heart?"

2

SHIPWRECKED

The harsh wind blew across the river. Rhys, trembling with cold, hunched down in the boat to protect himself from it.

He kept his eye on the river, watching for snags and banks hidden just under the surface of the water. There was no fear of being caught by the Belmarch by now. He had left them behind days ago, but he had no help if he ran aground, and the water was freezing. Splashes of it, and spray, flew in his face and froze into thin icicles off his eyebrows and his beard.

The current was swift and was sweeping him downstream at an astounding pace. Using an oar as a stiller, he turned the boat around the river bends.

As he turned the small amount of water in the bottom of the boat sloshed and splashed at his feet. His legs were getting tired, he was propping them up out of the water. Every so often he had to stop and scoop a few more inches out of the boat to toss over the side with a small bucket.

The boat was leaking. There wasn't anything he could do about it now, it wasn't fast and he didn't have any way to repair it. The sawdust stuffed into the joints held up somewhat, swelling to fill the void, but the pressure of the water beneath the boat was pushing it out. He was having to do more bailing and less watching, and it made him nervous.

And the wind wasn't helping. It pushed the surface of the water up into waves that rocked and cracked against the boat's hull, setting him on edge. His teeth clamped together tightly, his hand white, gripping the edge of the oar.

The bank was covered in forest, but the river was high and the edges of the bank jagged and rocky. He had thought about stopping and walking the rest of the way, but each time he thought of the others waiting for him, starving to death, he kept going.

With a plish, a clump of sawdust gave way. Water streamed into the boat. Rhys cursed, looked up at the stars, and wondered where he was.

Sweat broke out on his brow, making him even colder, and he bailed furiously. It wasn't enough though, he couldn't keep up.

Just one more bend, then I'll have to get to the bank. It had been so long since he had been on the river, years if not decades, but the moon glimmering in the reflection shattered into a million pieces by the wind.

His heart was beating a mile a minute and thundered in his ears. His shirt and coat were wet, and he shivered with the cold. He couldn't wait any longer and aimed for the bank.

A ripple, a hump caught his eye, and he reacted without thinking. Rhys turned the boat back into the middle of the river.

Something scraped against the hull, then popped as it reached the back of the hull. The boat lurched rightward, tilting so much it almost threw Rhys off.

He couldn't control it. The boat was listing heavily to the right, and a quick glance told him it was over. The hull had a deep gash ripped in it below the waterline.

All he could do now was pray and bail, hoping it would hold up enough to make it to the bank.

Rhys bailed furiously, his arms protesting against the use. The flaps of skin on his arms jiggled in his sleeves.

The boat struck the bank. Rhys lurched forward, falling into the water with a splash. His entire skin contracted it was so cold, and he came out of it spluttering and splashing.

He reached back, grabbed his pack, and struggled to get out onto the muddy bank. The river roared in his ears, and the boat started to creak and groan.

He made it, scrambling up the bank on his hands and knees, and stopped at the top, gasping for breath. It was colder than ever, and he knew he was in danger. He was starting to feel sleepy and struggled to his feet.

Leaving the boat behind, Rhys turned south and walked, forcing each leg forward even though they protested.

He wasn't sure how long he walked, but the sky was beginning to brighten. His mind was a fog, and he couldn't think well. Had he gone far enough downriver to Jareth?

There was shouting, or something like it, in the distance. Rhys kept walking, trudging, and stumbling. He kept getting back to his feet, and his lips were moving.

Hands grabbed at him, pulled him up over shoulders. Someone was looking at him, talking to him, but he was so far away.

Rhys wanted to close his eyes and go to sleep, but rough hands shook at him.

A door opened, light flowing out of it, and Rhys passed through. It was warm inside, but it made him shiver more. Something was at his lips, and he drank of it. It wasn't cold, but it wasn't hot either.

They laid him down, and then, at last, Rhys slipped off to sleep.

"We should move now and risk the river." General Granb stared over the table with a glare, daring others to speak.

"You wish to throw away our fighters? Waste them without purpose?" Sable sneered. "It is no wonder we've had such a hard time lately. No, we know the siege is strong and the castle is weak. It would be prudent to invade later, once the river subsides."

Raltone rubbed his chin, then let them bicker for another few minutes, enjoying the back and forth.

Granb was getting quite worked up, his face red. The scars stood out even whiter than usual. They were shouting at each other now.

"Enough," Raltone said, waving a hand. The noise died down. He couldn't hide the irritation in his voice. "The castle was supposed to be mine months ago. That was your responsibility, General Granb."

"It was Shigon that failed you," Granb said, the color draining from his face. "He was too weak to overpower a minimal amount of troops and a bunch of tradesmen."

"Silence," Raltone hissed. Granb shut his mouth quickly, almost taking a step back. He wouldn't let this ruin his plans. "These Chathem will pay for their resistance, and they will serve as an example of what happens to those that resist us."

He slammed a fist onto the table. "For too long you have all failed me. I grow tired of it."

Silence fell, a deadly silence. Raltone scowled at them all. "Chathem will be ours."

Rhys awoke to the sound of voices, hushed and low. When he opened his eyes, he was confused. This was a strange place, a place he did not know.

"Where-" he coughed at the effort of trying to speak, his voice catching in his parched throat.

His body wasn't responding how he wanted it to.

"Drink this," a woman's voice said. Something hard was held to his lips, then clear, sweet water flowed into his mouth. "We almost lost you to the cold stranger."

Rhys sat up, with some help from the woman and a man next to her. He was in a bed in a small cabin. It smelled of fish, in a good way, and woodsmoke.

A fire crackled merrily in the corner fireplace. The sight of it almost made him cry. The cold that settled in his bones was gone, and he soaked up the heat.

"Where am I?" he asked.

"Greenport," the man said. His eyes were hard and piercing, a strange contrast to the woman's warm gaze. "Who are you?" he demanded.

"Poppy," the woman scolded. "We talked about this. The poor man's almost up and died."

"I understand. I'm Rhys Clayton, once courtier to the King and Overseer of Castle Hornblood's construction." The words sapped the strength out of him.

Poppy's eyes didn't unharden. "Never heard of no Castle Hornblood around here, or any castle."

"Excuse my husband, dear. You came in looking like a ghost last night, and you don't look much better. Would you like something to eat?"

The mention of food made his mouth water, then he smelled it. Butter. Real butter, and milk. Fresh bread was mixed in with it and nearly drove him crazy with desire.

"Yes, yes!" Rhys cried.

They helped him to the table, and he fell upon the bowl of butter. It melted in his mouth, rich and creamy, sliding down like smooth silk into his ravenous stomach. When he had emptied the bowl, he turned his attention to the milk.

They stared at him like they would a wild animal. He didn't care at first, but when his appetite began to fade, he slowed and tried to regain his composure.

He looked around for something to wipe his face but found none. Something dribbled down his beard, so he tried to wipe it away.

Watching his saviors, he felt a sense of shame come over him at his actions. "I apologize for my rudeness. It's-" he started again. "The castle is starving. I haven't had a good meal in weeks." He tried to sound nonchalant, but he hid the fact he hadn't eaten since he boarded the boat days ago. He couldn't bear to take anything else with him, even though they had packed food with his supplies. He had left it in the kitchen when no one was looking.

"I see," Poppy said, even though he didn't look like he saw at all. His wife elbowed him in the ribcage.

"We forgot to introduce ourselves," she said. "My name is Pike, and this is my husband, Poppy. I function as a sort of healer in the village, so it was no wonder they brought you to my doorstep."

"Pleased to make your acquaintance," Rhys said. "How far are we from the capital?"

"Ironwood? Ain't much more than a few days' ride in good weather," Poppy said, scratching his chin.

Rhys tried to stand, but he was weak and fell back again. Pike let out a small cry of alarm and rushed to his side.

"What are you doing? You'll hurt yourself." They eased him back into the chair, stiff backed and hard.

"I have to get to the capital," Rhys said. "You don't understand, I have to get there as soon as I can." He clutched at their arms, looking from one to the other. "If we don't send help, they're going to die."

"You're in no shape to be going anywhere," Poppy said, pulling him over to the bed.

"You need your rest, dear," Pike said, eyes creased with concern. Rhys struggled, trying to break free, but he was too weak. His breath came short, and he started coughing again.

They eased him back into the bed. Rhys gripped at Pike's arm, his thin fingers clutched around her wrist. "I have to make it there, tonight, as soon as possible."

She gave him a pained smile. "That won't be possible. It's snowing now. A big blizzard is moving in."

He stopped and listened. The wind was howling outside, and there were drifts of snow spilling through cracks around the door and oilcloth windows. He hadn't realized it until then, the sound of the fire had been too loud.

The thought of going out into the cold again, after being so warm, made him shudder, and brought with it a heaping of shame.

He should go anyway. Everyone in the castle was going to have to deal with this, why should he be any different?

Rhys took a deep breath. The smell of dinner was still thick, but his stomach was so full he feared eating anything else would cause it to burst. That satisfaction brought more shame with it, piling on more.

"Is there no one who could take me?"

"I don't think you'd get anyone tonight," Poppy said.

Rhys worked his jaw, finally speaking at last. "The more time I take, the more people die. I must reach the capital. Will you help me?"

3

Cold Water Fishing

"Will you tell us about them?" Pike sat down on a stool next to the bed. Rhys let go of her arm and put it over his eyes.

"About a hundred men, women, and children are stuck, trapped in a siege. We've been building a fortification for over three years at the headwaters of the Golden River, a bastion to protect us from Belmarch."

He couldn't meet their eyes. "But we weren't fast enough. They came on us in the night, burning and looting, and we were forced to retreat into the castle. They tried to take it, and we repelled them time and time again, and now they seem content to starve us out. They sent me, risking all, to get help."

The house was silent except for the wind and fire. There was a tapping on the side of the door, a rattle of wood on wood.

Pike sat, chewing her lip. Poppy took out a pipe and slowly packed it, getting up to take a stick from the fire to light it. He stood there, puffing out great plumes of white.

"You bring us ill news," Pike said, breaking the silence. "We haven't heard of any of this."

"Will you help me? I have friends, well-connected friends, that will reward any who help me. Belmarch is on the rise, and if we don't stop them, we could be swept away." Rhys was feeling his strength fade away. They were right, he couldn't leave tonight if he wanted to. "I'm in no shape to travel, I agree with you, but it might be that there would be someone who could take me as far as Jareth."

Poppy cleared his throat and looked at Pike. No words passed between them, but he turned to a peg on the wall where his coat and hat hung and put them on. "Stay here, I'll ask around."

"In the meantime, you need to get some rest," Pike said. "I'll make you some tea to help you get to sleep."

As she got up to put the kettle on Poppy knocked out his pipe into the fire, red ash that licked up like a fiery snow. He opened the door, a wild wind bringing with it gusts of snow, struggled outside, and slammed it shut behind him.

Rhys let go of Pike and slipped back into the bed. His thoughts and emotions churned like the blizzard outside, tossing this way and that.

What am I going to do? He wanted to go out into the cold, continue his journey. He needed to, the weight of it hung on his shoulders like irons.

But he couldn't make it like this. He knew that, and so did they. Now he was reliant on the kindness of strangers to accomplish his mission.

Do I need to do it? Would anyone fault me for giving up? Rhys turned uncomfortably at the thought.

He could do it, go south and drift into obscurity. He might spend his next few months running, but there were places beyond the reach of the Chathem King. Many places, and no one knew he had escaped the castle except the defenders inside.

It would be so easy to run from his duty, to let the burden slip off and fall into the river. They were almost dead anyway, and he owed them nothing.

"What is it?" Pike asked, at his side in an instant. "You seem so troubled."

"Nothing," Rhys said quickly.

"I saw it in your eyes, tell me." She was young, the wrinkles not touching her eyes yet. They looked at him, first at one eye then the other.

"I think of my companions, that is all." *You didn't tell her that you were thinking of abandoning them to their fate, did you? You're a weak man, unworthy of any title.*

"Why does it trouble you so?" Pike was staring at him, like he was emitting some kind of strange light.

"Are they your friends?"

"Hardly. A man of my station-" What station was he now? An Overseer who abandoned his post? Royal blood without any prospects? "I'm tired. I must rest now." Rhys turned away, pulling the thick, woolen blanket up around his shoulders.

Pike respected his wishes and left him alone, but it didn't make Rhys satisfied. His exhausted body, finally filled with food for the first time in months, forced him into a fitful and troubled sleep.

Rhys woke guilty and in a strange place. It was daytime, or just barely, a tinge of red cast on the log wall of the cabin. Someone was at the fire, poking it and bringing it back to life, even as the wind howled through the eaves.

He was hungry, but somehow warm. Rhys sat up, letting the thick blanket slip and a tinge of the cool air in the cabin touch him. He quickly wrapped it around his body.

"Good morning," Pike said, smiling. She was busy in the small kitchen near the fireplace, mixing something in a big wooden bowl. Her arm moved furiously, but she seemed completely serene otherwise.

"Good morning," Rhys said, swinging his legs over the side of the bed and touching them to the cool floorboards.

"Morning," Poppy said, stirring the fire and adding another log. It smashed into the ashes, sending up a flurry of red and yellow that burned out immediately.

"Are you feeling better this morning?" Pike asked. She spooned out a measure of the mixture into a pan and set it on the coals that Poppy had revealed.

Rhys examined his body, and tested his muscles. Everything seemed to be in good working order, if not a touch sore. Other than his hunger, which wasn't sure he could ever satisfy again, nothing seemed out of place. He had even slept better than he had in weeks, even distressed as he was.

"I'm much better, thank you." Rhys winced. "I apologize for my ill manners. I wasn't... myself yesterday."

"You've had a dreadful burden to carry, dear. Don't worry your head about it. Once we fill up your belly with my flatcakes you'll feel right as rain."

"Is there any word on the...help?" Rhys asked. He stood, moved closer to the warmth of the fire, catching a glimpse of outside.

It was covered in snow, still and quiet except for the wind. The world was hazy through the oilcloth covering the openings, even though ice crept in the corners. He was grateful of the fire as soon as he saw it, and the snow at the edges of the door. It was impossible to keep the weather out, and was a reminder of the castle and the people depending on him.

"Are you sure you're up to traveling?" Pike asked, brow creased and wrinkled.

"I don't have a choice. I have to go. I must go." Rhys sat at the table.

"Joe's got a sled and horses. He said he could do it, but didn't seem keen on it." Poppy joined him at the table and took out a pipe, packing the bowl slowly.

"Do put that away, Poppy. Let him alone."

"I don't mind," Rhys said. "Please, go ahead." *I won't be any more of an inconvenience than I already am.* Pike took out the first of the cakes, golden brown and smelling wonderful, and added another batch. In another pot she dropped a few eggs into boiling water, watching them almost as much as she watched Rhys.

"We've managed to find some clothes your size," Pike nodded to the foot of the bed. "You'll have to excuse them. They aren't in the best condition, but you need them."

They looked tired and worn, but far warmer than what he had on now. While breakfast was cooking he put them on. They were a little large for him in his current condition.

"Thank you, these are an improvement. I don't deserve your kindness," Rhys said, joining Poppy as he puffed on the pipe and sent lazy spirals of tobacco smoke wafting around the small cabin. Half of it was sucked out of the cabin immediately through the drafts, but the rest hung to the rafters above.

Pike announced breakfast, and Rhys licked his lips. His mouth had been watering the entire time she had been cooking, and he tore into the food as soon as it touched his plate, although with more restraint than he had the previous evening.

"Slow down, you might choke," Poppy said with an arched eyebrow.

"Let him be. He's still almost half dead," Pike chided. The food was delicious, the flatcakes warm and fluffy, a crunchy crust with a soft, puffy inside, and the eggs were cooked until they were firm but still soft.

Even as he ate it and enjoyed it, a wave of shame washed over him. Here he was, stuffing his face, while others starved.

But he had to eat. He wouldn't have strength for anything if he didn't. Like it or not, he had to do it.

"When is the earliest he can leave, this Joe?" Rhys asked between bites. He knew it wasn't proper of him, but he couldn't help it. He had already wasted too much time as it was.

"I don't know." Poppy was short and to the point. "He didn't promise he'd do it. It would be mighty inconvenient for him to do it at all, let alone now."

"I have resources."

Poppy's eyebrows raised. "Do you now?"

"Not with me," Rhys confessed. He could convince them to empty the treasury, if it would stop the Belmarch at the border. *I think.*

"That makes it a might harder to take you seriously, then." Poppy took a bite of his flatcake. "And Joe a lot more reluctant to go."

"The Belmarch have already invaded," Rhys said, wiping the last of his plate clean with a piece of cake and devouring it. "When they sweep through here, killing and burning, will Joe take that as currency?"

Pike looked at Poppy. They exchanged an uneasy glance, and Poppy returned the pipe to his mouth with a click of his teeth. His smoke cut through the smell of breakfast.

"I've no reason to lie about it." Rhys stood up, rolled up his sleeve, and grabbed a bit of his hanging flesh, pulling it so tight they could see the bone underneath. "Do you think a man wants to be like this for pleasure?"

"We don't think you're lying," Pike said. "It's just that we're a simple folk in a simple place. What you say is... complicated."

"It'll be simple enough when the blood starts flowing." Rhys sat back down. "This isn't something you can avoid, and you know it."

"They've never come down this far before," Pike said, but there was a hint of concern in her voice.

"I'll take him," Poppy said.

"Poppy, you can't do that."

"Someone has to. I don't see Joe doing it anytime soon without payment up front. That only leaves one other option."

"Whoever takes me, we need to leave soon. The sooner the better." The food had given Rhys some of his strength back. He thought he could make it now, provided he would still be able to eat. *But what about them?*

"I don't like it." Pike shook her head. "Not one bit." She sighed. "But I see you've made up your mind. Easier to break a rock than change it. I'll help you get ready."

Poppy nodded and tapped out his pipe into the fire. "I'll get the sled ready."

4

At the Mercy of Others

A few hours later, and after a hearty lunch that continued to restore him to health, Rhys found himself atop a homemade sled in two feet of snow. A brown mare was hitched to it, breath streaming out her nostrils like smokestacks.

It was another cold day that took the breath away, but Rhys was better protected now with thicker clothes and a warmer, if worn, coat.

"Take care of him," Pike called, waving from the doorway, a shawl wrapped around her shoulders. Poppy nodded, but Rhys wasn't sure she was talking to Poppy or him. He had thanked her for her kindness, and for saving his life, but he wasn't sure it had been enough.

He was still feeling weak, and coughed as he eyed the horizon and sky. It was clear, but this was the time of year where that was little solace against the winter snowstorms that came in without notice.

"We'll be fine," Poppy said, taking up the reins. Rhys nodded, and the man whipped the mare into action. The sled groaned, then skimmed over the snow as the horse kicked great gouts of it up with her footsteps.

"To Jareth, then the capital," Rhys murmured.

"Unless we cross now, head west."

"We? I couldn't ask you to do that. I'll find a way when I get to Jareth," Rhys said, bumping along with the rest of the supplies. Pike had loaded them down with enough to last for weeks, as well as enough firewood that it almost over-burdened the horse. Poppy had removed some, despite her protests, but there was plenty left.

"Do you think there's even enough snow to make it the whole way?" Rhys asked. The sled skimmed over the surface of the fresh snow, the mare struggling through the deep piles of it.

"More than enough. I know a way." Poppy barely held the reins, twitching them every so often if the horse strayed from his intended path.

"I told you; I can find a way myself." The last thing Rhys wanted to do was find himself more in debt to these people. They had saved him, kept him alive, and now were willing to take him where he needed to go.

The sun came out, sparkling on the snow like stars. It was so bright it hurt his eyes, so he hid them.

"And how would you do that?" Poppy pulled out his pipe and put it between his teeth, keeping it unlit. His hood was so big it nearly touched his mustache. "Exchange your non-ex-istent coin for a ride?"

Rhys stewed it over in his mind. He hadn't been prepared for this, or not nearly enough. All that time he had thought the biggest problem would be getting out of the castle.

He sniffed. "I see your point. I'm reliant on the kindness of strangers."

"Is that what we are now?"

"That isn't what I meant. I-" They passed by a copse of trees, then entered a meadow. The snow was shallower here, and the horse snorted and pulled ahead at a faster trot. "You've already done too much for me. It isn't right to ask you to do more."

"Good thing I'm not asking." Poppy leaned back, pulled his hat almost over his eyes to block the glare. "Besides, Pike needs some things we can't get out here. A trip to Ironwood wouldn't hurt. And I have healing tonics she needs to sell."

He motioned behind him. The tinkling that Rhys had heard was a group of bottles in a straw filled box at the top of the supplies.

Rhys looked back at him. "You talked it over with her, didn't you?"

Poppy shrugged. "You were sleeping all night and half the morning. We had to talk about something."

"And I suppose you said I wouldn't make it on my own."

Poppy shrugged, took his pipe from his mouth and tapped it over the side of the sled.

"Well," Rhys said after a while. "Thank you."

The air was cold, almost frighteningly so, but he was warm. It felt like a miracle. The wind from the sled whipped across his cheeks, providing a light sting, but it almost felt refreshing after spending so much time outside. Rhys lifted his head to the sky and closed his eyes. He let the sun soak into his cheeks, counteracting the tinge of cold with a tingle of warmth. His lip twitched, and he almost smiled at it.

There was a good chance he could do it. With Poppy to lead him they would make it to Ironwood, and then Whitehall.

He could picture it now, the great gleaming walls of mottled white stone rising higher than any building in the building, supported by massive blocks of stone at the base that got progressively lighter as they went up. The King would be standing at the lattice windows, watching him coming, his court surrounding him, vying for attention.

And Rhys would be back in his element.

He almost shivered at it, thinking of the intrigue and drama that must have exchanged while he was gone on his exile to the northern lands.

That small thing came back into his mind, a mere trifle that threatened to overpower everything else. He could let them go, let them meet their fate. He could return to his riches, his satin and down pillows, warmed for him by servants.

Another nagging through pricked at him, the memory of faces. Sick, cold faces half-starved, some of them children. It overpowered them quickly.

Each face was a chain, fastened around his neck. Each one weighed him down, returned him to his duty.

He had taken the position of Overseer of the Castle Horn-blood unwillingly, forced out by chance and machinations of others. However, he had sworn an oath to do his duty and execute the will of his King and people.

Rhys shivered and pulled his coat tighter around his neck. The sled bumped over something harder than the snow, making a heart wrenching grating noise.

"If you've got something on your mind best let it out now," Poppy said beside him. The reins were in his lap now, the mare seemed to know the way on her own. He was calmly filling his pipe full of tobacco leaf. "We've a long road ahead of us, several days."

The cold in his heart overwhelmed the warmth of the sun and the sparkle of the snow. The landscape looked fresh and clean, but his heart was too full and heavy.

"Given enough time, yes. Right now..." Rhys shrugged.

"Suit yourself." They traveled over the snow, out of familiar lands. The sound of the river had long faded away, only the sound of the sled and the jingle of the harness on the horse made any noise now.

Rhys leaned back, closed his eyes, and slipped off into sleep.

His face was cold when the sled pulled to a halt, waking him. Rhys opened his eyes, blinking in the light of the late morning sun.

The landscape had changed. The rolling hills and spindly trees had given way to plains. Looking closer, Rhys realized that there were houses dotting the horizon, and barns.

"Where are we?" His voice cracked, unused to going so long without use. Poppy reached down beside him and pulled out a waterskin and handed it to him.

"Drink up. We've left the river lands behind. Now we're in the heart of Chathem, farmland and plains as far as you can see." Poppy turned and dug around in the supplies while Rhys drank greedily.

The second it hit his lips the water shocked him with how cold it was, chunks of ice mixed in. He drank it, feeling relief from the thirst that had shown itself when he had recovered from waking. It gathered in his belly until it had warmed.

"This is the Chathem I'm most familiar with."

"Oh?" Poppy turned, a lump of cheese and some bread fished from behind him. He handed it off to Rhys and took a small carrot and bag of grains to the horse, who was breathing heavily.

They were beside a small creek, frozen over in the winter air, and after a few kicks from Poppy's boot, accessible to the horse to drink from.

"I grew up in a place like it."

"On a farm?"

"No." Rhys stood up, stretching the soreness out of his muscles. His joints popped as he did, and he groaned. "Not a farm. Where did you grow up?"

"Right near the river," Poppy said. "My father was a bargeman, did some time traveling, and settled down with my mother where we live now." He peered up into the sky, then crunched across the snow to take the rest of the food.

It was good, and the cheese went well with the bread. Poppy tore off a piece of bread and popped it into his mouth.

"You stayed."

"I had to. The river is in my blood, in many."

"You couldn't leave if you wanted to. Even to take a poor beggar halfway across the kingdom." Rhys spread out his hands.

Poppy smiled. "You might say that. I've done my fair share of traveling too. Can't say I like it as much as staying home." Poppy went back to his side of the sled. "Well and good. Ready?"

Rhys nodded, then sat back down as he flicked the reins. Butter, the mare, took off at a light trot. The snow was thinner here, but still came up above her ankles.

They didn't talk much the rest of the day. Rhys watched the world go by, watching the farmers come to their doors and look back at them.

Their stoves sent white spirals of smoke up in the air, eventually mingling with the clouds up above.

Rhys thought. He wondered who he would go to first. He thought about what he would say. He thought about who to avoid.

There were all too many of the latter. Oh, if he could go back in time and do it all again, he would, and better.

Much better.

"We'll stop for dinner," Poppy said.

"How long will Butter go?"

"She'll go for a while. Don't worry, we'll get there in time."

"I'm not sure we will, even if we travel all night." The wind was harsh against his face, and there was no protection here, no groups of trees to break it, even if it was poor cover. The gaunt faces, the thin as reeds arms and legs lingered in his mind.

Poppy looked at him with a searching eye. "No use to worry about what you can't change. You'll doubt yourself to death if you think that way."

Rhys furrowed his brows. "I'd rather not speak of death."

"Ah, but death will come whether you speak of it or not." Poppy clicked and pulled up the reins. "Here is as good as any."

Rhys stewed in his own thoughts as they ate, hating that there wasn't more he could do. The meal was brief, and light, and left him wanting more.

The sun was going down now, slipping beneath the horizon without a hint of sunset on a cloudless sky. After so many days of winter, it was a relief to have so little cloud cover.

They started back again, with the horse going at little more than a brisk walk. Rhys couldn't get out and pull it himself, but he felt like if he did it wouldn't be much slower.

They made light conversation, talking about the weather and the river. Boats were a common topic for both of them, and Rhys remembered enough about them to keep the conversation flowing.

"You seem to know a lot about boats for a man who grew up on a farm."

"Near farms, not on one," Rhys said. "And I didn't say I stayed there, only that it was where I grew up. I felt a calling to the river and ended up at a port town of some importance."

"Jareth?"

"No. It doesn't matter. I learned enough to keep me in knowledge until now, apparently, but not so much to make me a master at it. Life circumstances changed, and that road led me here."

5

AT THE EDGE

Evan considered himself in the pale reflection of the mirror. He touched his cheeks, sunken in more than he'd ever seen them.

His stomach growled at him, the constant nagging hunger that seemed to gnaw him from the inside ever present. Evan coughed. The cold hadn't eased up in weeks, and the wind howled around the Keep outside.

He pulled his coat tighter and left his room and the Keep. Along the way he greeted the few who were up and about. They bowed and gave him deference, but not like they used to.

Evan hurt inside each time it happened. *Who am I, that I deserve it though?* He was lucky to still be alive, considering everything that had happened.

The wind bit his nose and face as the door to the Keep almost flew out of his hands. Bracing himself, Evan walked out into the cold.

A foot and a half of snow coated the courtyard, in the places it hadn't drifted up against the walls and the buildings in the castle. The sun, obscured by the clouds, cast little light. They were coming off the shortest days, but not by much.

He should be walking among the garrison, inspecting his men before they took to the walls for duty. Instead, few men dotted the walls, too few, but there was too little food to expect them up there in this weather.

The snow squelched underfoot as he walked through the path that others had trodden down. He had a destination in mind and walked with determination.

The guards in the guardhouse tried to snap to attention when he walked in, and it pleased him, but their movements were weak and they barely rose from sitting positions, or leaned up from lying.

"Duke, good morning. I wasn't expecting you," Mathew said. He wasn't Evan's first choice, but Rhys had vouched for him, and it was enough to give him a chance.

Not that Evan had much of a choice.

"Please, as you were," Evan said. Looks of relief flooded faces, and they sat down with a groan, as if there was a big rush of air in the building. It was surprisingly warm inside, except near the door, and Evan moved into the room to escape the cold.

How he wished for a fire again. "I've come to see how everyone is." Evan walked along the rows of bunks. Faces stared at him, exhausted and gaunt. Arms were thin, and so were legs. Mathew followed him nervously. "Relax guardsman, I'm not here to throw you out."

"I know that, Your Highness." Mathew glanced at his fellow guardsman and the workers that were slated for sentry duty. They were a pitiful lot. "May we speak in private?"

Evan completed his lap, surprised at how winded he was from his short excursion in the snow. He dreaded going outside, but there was nowhere more private at the time.

"They look tired," Evan noted.

"We're sleeping all the time. The rations are too low, we need more food." Mathew spoke with boldness, his clothes hanging off his body. "Some of the men are grumbling. They don't think Rhys survived the attack, they say he was killed by an arrow."

Evan was swept back for a moment, to the moment he saw Rhys and his boat slip out of his sight. The man looked alive but bent down to avoid the very fate Mathew mentioned. "Have faith. The trip downriver was a few days, and a week or more to get to the capital. Rhys will do his duty and bring us help." Evan spoke with more conviction than he felt, another doubt that seemed to gnaw at him. *Should I have gone myself?*

He imagined himself riding into Whitehall, astride his steed. He would have dismounted and swept into the throne room, to the surprise of all those in attendance, and demanded an immediate audience with the King.

The vision dissolved and vanished. That was not to be, it was never to be.

"It's just..."

"Go on," Evan urged.

"They should have been here by now, if they were coming." the capital was a few weeks away by foot, but he was right. Had they moved immediately they would have been here.

Weeks ago.

"Have faith," Evan said, repeating words he had heard his father say during difficult times. "We will see the end of this." *True words, however they turn out.*

"You're right, Your Highness." Mathew seemed mollified, if for the moment. Would this conversation spread?

"Send word if you need any help." What he meant went unspoken, of course. They needed help, lots of it. Whether it would come or not, Evan could only guess. "I will be up on the wall for the next few minutes."

Mathew acknowledged and saluted him, then went back inside.

Evan turned back to the wall. The steps were mostly free of ice, but there were some trickier parts that required extra attention. He had been doing rounds of the battlements ever since Rhys had left, and it seemed to be helping.

He was getting to know them men, at least. Their names, for starters, something he never would have thought about a few months ago, but something his father had urged him to do.

"Get to know your men and they will fight harder for you. Show that you care." Words spoken long ago, in what seemed like a different life.

Time seemed to rush by and creep slowly all at once. One minute he was thinking how slow the day was going and then the next minute a week had passed.

Not having enough food had contributed. His training sessions had shortened, then stopped. Now he spent most of his time reading through the library of books, even the boring ones, and walking through the castle.

He did the same today, stopping at each sentry to see how he was doing and if he had seen anything of note. Each man, and there were about five in all, said no to the latter and put up a good show about the former, but they all shivered and didn't have enough clothes for how cold it was.

They shared the coats. Evan had found that out quite by accident one day. He wished they didn't have to, and had demanded his servants search the store rooms for extra clothes, but there was none to be had. Most of them were lost in the initial attack, leaving little for the others to wear.

He should have thought about that when he came up here. He should have planned better, made them bring everything inside the walls.

Yand had urged him to do it, and he let the Overseer's worry about moving everything slowing down the construction overrule the good advice. He was hoping Rhys would make up for it now, but that nagging worry that he was already dead filled him with dread.

Evan pulled his cloak closer, painfully aware of how much more it protected him than the other men on the wall. He gazed out toward the smoke of the Belmarch camp. They were warming themselves around the fire, laughing and talking as if they were having a feast and not conducting a siege. Their voices drifted up to him over the cold, snowy plain that separated them.

The ruins of the village were hidden by the white blanket that covered everything. They still sent sentries to the woods every day. The Belmarch weren't letting their guard down at all.

But Evan felt like theirs was slipping. While he was up on the wall another batch of men came out of the guardhouse and up the stairs, taking the watch from the freezing men and transferring bows, arrows, and coats.

Another thing to worry about, the supply of arrows and bowstrings. Evan chewed his lip as he watched them carelessly transfer from frozen fingers to frozen fingers. One slip and the strings would be lost in the snow and ruined.

He couldn't do anything about it. *What would I do, yell at them?* They fumbled, exhausted from lack of food, but none were lost in the exchange. It was a small miracle.

Once more he looked to the south, straining his eyes on the horizon, hoping and praying he would see an army marching through the forest on their way to rescue them.

For a second, he could almost hear the tramp of feet, hear the cadence being called out and repeated.

But it was all in his mind. There were no troops. There might not be anyone coming.

Are they waiting for spring? The snow would pose a challenge to any force big enough to bring them what they needed. Food, supplies, clothing, arms, Evan had no doubt Rhys would have them bring what they needed.

If Rhys even made it. Evan blinked as the sun came out from behind the clouds, bringing a hint of blessed warmth but shining bright in his eyes. Evan couldn't stand being up on the wall and walked down the icy steps and back to the Keep.

No longer a prisoner in his own quarters, Evan didn't feel like he had free rein of the castle.

He didn't want to go back, but the wind was too harsh and the cold too biting to do anything but seek shelter, so Evan slunk back to the Keep and slipped inside.

It wasn't warm or cozy, but inside he was able to get out of the wind. It helped. Evan rubbed some life back into his limbs and went back through the corridor to the great room, pausing to look around.

Over in the corner someone coughed. Evan frowned at it, and how ill it sounded. He hoped it wouldn't spread like the plagues he was reading about.

When his eyes adjusted, they were met with a sad sight. The mattresses, or what served as the mattresses, were pushed together in a big heap. Bodies piled up against each other to conserve warmth, and the coughs ran through the pile.

Forms shifted, eyes peered up at him. Faces, gaunt with hunger, seared into his mind. Some of them were children.

They had lost a little boy last week. Evan had watched them carry the body out into the cold to be set to freeze. The ground was too hard to dig into even if they had the strength. It joined the growing pile set aside for warmer weather to deal with.

How much longer will they last? Evan looked away, unable to bear it, knowing that he bore the brunt of the responsibility. He should have anticipated this better and pushed for a stronger garrison when he had the chance.

Now all he could do was sit and wait, hope that Rhys had made it.

He returned to his study, and stood beneath the large crest above his desk. It wasn't the best he had seen, there were craftsmen in the capital that would make a wooden bird seem real, but it was honest and well made with an even hand.

Unlike himself, it represented the best of his line. The Tree unbroken by winter and wind, an ever present landmark on the horizon. He recalled how it swayed and moved in the summer breezes, and towered over all other trees in winter, thick and fat in comparison to the twigs around it.

He took out the Histories and grabbed a blanket, wrapping it around himself as he sunk into the chair.

It creaked and protested, but not because of his weight. Something about the air seemed to suck the strength out of everything, living and unliving, in the castle.

He tried to read, but his mind wandered, distracted. Evan got up and walked around, pacing his room to get his blood flowing, until at last dinner was brought in.

Barger had brought it, and after a pleasant greeting stood waiting for Evan to dismiss him.

For some reason he couldn't. Evan caught sight of Barger's wrists in his sleeves. They were so thin and bony he mistook them for twigs.

"Is everything all right, Your Highness?"

Evan stared at the wrists, then back to his plate. It was the usual, mush heaped up in a little pile, but something kept nagging at him.

He felt his own wrists, poked at them with a bony finger. He had never been plump himself, but he still had muscle to spare.

All at once he made the connection, and it angered him. Evan pushed away his plate and turned back to his servant.

His eyes burned with passion, his sadness consumed. "You have been giving me more than the ration, haven't you?"

6

THE SECRET

Barger stood, eyes wide, before an angry Duke of Hornblood.

"Yes, Your Highness." He bowed his head, answering Evan at last. He didn't want to , Evan could see it in his eyes.

"Who gave this order?" Evan stood, almost knocking back his chair. The little one had died of hunger, of that he was sure, and here he was eating more than his share.

"The Overseer told us to. He said you needed your strength for what was to come."

He had a fair point. If Evan wasted away, who would be left to lead them? Thinking about it sent a sharp stab of shame.

After all he had done, he deserved no special treatment. As he turned it over in his mind, he wondered if he didn't deserve less for all his inaction.

"Rhys," he growled, pacing the room. "I should have known." A thought came to him. Evan spun on his heel. "What else have you been hiding from me?"

"I hid nothing, Your Highness," Barger said, his tone conciliatory. "The Overseer never told us to lie either."

"But you did."

"No, Your Highness."

Evan wanted to shout at him, he wanted to hit him, he wanted to do something to the pitiful wretch, but the more his passion flowed the more he knew he couldn't. This wasn't Barger's fault. It wasn't even Rhys' fault.

It was his own.

The food seemed like a curse was on it. *How am I supposed to eat it now?* He wished he had never seen it, never thought about it.

But that wasn't right either. The stores were getting so low they were down to the moldy and rotten dregs of the harvests. They had weeks, at most, left, perhaps even less.

Or that was what he was told.

Fear crept up his spine. A deep dread crept into his soul, and he wondered if the inventories he had been given were right.

"Take it back, give it to the most needful." Barger started to protest but Evan cut him off. He picked up his cloak and fastened it back on. "I'm going to the cellars and I don't want you or anyone else to stop me."

Evan marched out of the door and down the hall, but then his steps faltered. He hadn't been down to the cellars since he arrived. He didn't know where they were. *Are they behind the great hall in the kitchen?*

Chewing his lip, Evan slowed his pace to a crawl. He had never taken the time to explore the castle before, not beyond the easy and obvious places. The kitchens, for instance, he had never been to.

He could ask, or he could find his own way. Evan thought of the looks he would get asking for directions for the food, so he made up his mind to find it by himself.

The obvious place to start were the stair towers, and so he went to the one nearest to his room and study, cracking open the door and heading down instead of up. It only went down one level before it ended, spitting him out into a dark, dank hall that was surprisingly warm through a small doorway.

His feet thudded on the rough stone floor, echoing in the empty hall. The walls were tight and there was barely enough room for him to move. It was hard to see and he let his eyes adjust to the light.

Evan wrinkled his nose. The smell down here was awful, a mixture of sewage, rot, and mold that he could barely stand. He covered his nose and moved forward, tracing one hand along the wall to keep from running into the wall.

His hand went over rough stone until it hit wood. Fumbling around, he finally found a metal door handle and pushed.

He realized why they hadn't been bringing him reports now. It was almost impossible to see anything but a big black shadow. It could have been a small room, a huge room, or anything in between for all he could tell.

I have to check. Evan held his breath and went in. He stumbled around in the dark, hoping his eyes would adjust, but the best he could see were strange shapes and the outline of the door he came in in gray.

"What am I doing here?" Evan stopped stumbling around the room and slipped to a sitting position. He was in an empty cellar in the unfinished castle his father had tasked him to complete, and all his subjects were starving to death.

He couldn't have messed it up any worse if he tried. All those years, all those lessons, all the harsh words, they were all for nothing. He banged his head against the wall, feeling the sharp lance of pain as it struck. *At least I feel something.*

His stomach growled at him, demanding more. Evan clutched at it with two hands. How many children felt the same, or worse, because he hadn't thought of asking a simple question? Or maybe he knew the whole time, deep down, and didn't care.

That would have been the old him, the Duke of Horn-blood known for his carousing and lack of morals. That Duke wouldn't have cared, not a single bit.

But he did. He felt shame, and sadness, that he hadn't seen earlier, hadn't asked earlier. It hurt. *Is this something I'm supposed to always feel?*

It was a burden, like a weight that had settled over his shoulders. It was crushing.

He wasn't sure how long he was down there, but Evan didn't really care. He went over his life, where he had gone wrong and what he could have done differently and wanted to.

Scenes of his youth replayed in his head. Nights he was ashamed of, that made him cringe inside even to this day. Guilt, shame, sadness, it all poured through him, infused into him.

He licked his lips, tasting the remnants of his morning meal, and it made him even more ashamed. The others hadn't had as much as he did. All those years he had wondered what it would be like to a commoner, and now, in this dark cell of a dungeon beneath a castle that was to be his, he felt it.

Hungry, alone, and guilt ridden, Evan mourned for a life that could have been.

He was roused only by the sound of the alarm bell, distant and distorted as it echoed through the halls and the stairs until it finally reached him. A stab of panic ran through him, and he jumped to his feet, tripping and tumbling in the darkness until he finally found the door.

We don't have the strength to resist them. Rough stone guided him left, then he saw the light from the stairs and rushed up it and back into his room.

His armor was ready, as it always was these days, and he rushed to put it on. The others would be manning the walls already, but it could be too late already.

Fatigue sapped him of his strength. The armor felt heavier than it really was, but there was nothing he could do about it now. After he strapped on his sword and took up his helmet, Evan ran to the door and out into the hallway.

There were still people asleep or huddled in the great hall as he passed it, but he paid no attention to them. The cold draft greeted him at the entrance door, and it was just as bad as he pushed them open into the dazzling light of the day.

When his eyes adjusted, he rushed over to the wall. He was right, it was lined with men. They looked tired, leaning on spears and against the walls, but all had their eyes trained on the enemy encampment to the south.

And they were all grouped on the southern walls.

Is it a feint? A surprise massing? Dread came up and filled his stomach as he took the stairs two at a time. It was still winter, and the Black River looked impassable to him, but there was always the chance the Belmarch would muster their forces and cross with an army that could crush them beneath their boots.

And it seemed that day had come.

"What's going on?" he asked as he got to the top, almost out of breath from the short journey. Mathew was standing near the gatehouse and was the only one to look back. Another pointed to the south.

Evan followed his hand. A lump formed in his throat, and his eyes burned.

He expected the sound of fighting, the twang of arrows, the clash of steel, but it had been too quiet. He realized that now and knew the reason.

The enemy camp had been deserted.

He blinked again, breath held, trying to fathom it. *The Belmarch had left.*

But that wasn't all, someone had taken their pace. Ranks of soldiers marched through the ruins of the makeshift village. Fifty, sixty, more. The sound of their boots reached them now.

"We're saved," someone said. The spell was broken, and reality acknowledged. The Tree of Everlong was held high on banners over the forces, and behind it looked to be wagons.

"Open the gate," Evan ordered, snapping out of his dream-like state that had come over him at the sight of it. "Everyone get to the gate."

He wasn't sure how they were going to open it, but he thought they might find a way. Cheers went up along the wall, men waving and shouting.

Then Evan realized it might be a trick. Men were already pouring down the wall though, eager to welcome the incoming forces. "Hold, don't open the gate," he yelled, going back to the edge of the wall. "Hold I said. Wait until we confirm."

That put a damper on the celebration. People were streaming out of the Keep, eager to see what the commotion was. Evan returned to the edge of the wall, casting a more dubious eye on the situation.

He cursed himself, not thinking of it sooner. It would have been like the Belmarch, devious and evil, to do something of the sort. He shook his head.

They had come so close to lowering their guard, letting them in without even checking. "Where are the sentries on the east and west walls?" Evan asked, turning back to Mathew.

"I-I don't know."

"Send men to them now, check to make sure we aren't being lured into a surprise attack." Evan caught himself, realizing that he wouldn't have even thought of this a few months ago, but he had read every book in the library now.

And more than one was about military tactics. Tactics such as fooling your enemies, posing as friendly forces to carry out sneak attacks.

But the more he looked upon the forces approaching the less he thought it was the case. He doubted himself, but the crest of the Hornbloods emblazoned on their banners were accurate, down to the branches on the tree.

"Sentries have been stationed on the east and west walls, Your Highness." Mathew had returned and was at his elbow now.

"Where is Freeman?" Evan asked.

"I haven't seen him."

"Get him up here." Mathew nodded and was off. Evan needed someone else with him who knew of this kind of thing. "Ready your bows, keep on the alert."

Bows were strung, and arrows readied, but the closer the soldiers got the more Evan thought that it really was them. They marched in ordered lines, each carrying a large pack on his back and enough armor to keep his vital organs covered but not too much to weigh him down.

He scanned the faces, but Evan didn't recognize anyone in the front ranks. They were looking up at the walls, and saw doubtful eyes looking back at them.

A man shouted an order, calling a halt. The group of soldiers stopped at once, in time, and stood. A tickle of some familiarity pulled at Evan, and he hoped beyond hope.

Was it him?

"Here, Your Highness." Sam Freeman was at his side now. "You wanted me?"

A quick glance caught Evan by surprise. Sam looked horrible, withered and pale. He quickly recomposed himself. "What do you think?"

A figure stepped out from the side of the group of the soldiers, head shrouded in a helmet. "They're well-armed," Sam said. "Over a hundred, I'd estimate." The figure approached the wall, tramping through the snow.

Evan kept a close eye on him. "Hold your arrows. He wants to talk." Bows lowered, arrows un-nocked. The figure stopped on the road below the gate.

"Since when was the Duke of Hornblood and his Captain so cautious?" The man yelled up to the wall. Evan let out a sigh of relief, hope and joy flowing through him now.

The man unfastened his helmet and took it off. Evan laughed at the confirmation, recognizing him immediately, then called down to him, "What a relief to see you, you old hound!"

7

A WELCOME CARAVAN

"You recognized me, I'm impressed." A grizzled face looked up at them, the hint of a smile playing at the corner of his mouth.

Evan laughed. "You know I'd recognize that voice, and who could forget a face like that?" A scar ran down the center of the man's face, not quite perfectly vertical, a souvenir from a dead general. "Open the gate," he called back.

"Glad you finally decided to show me some hospitality," the man said.

"Your Highness?" Sam asked.

"This is Captain Silverthorn, one of my father's oldest captains," Evan said. Sam nodded. Movement near the village caught his attention.

Wagons. And more than a few, there had to be a train of them. "Ah, I see you spotted the reason it took us so long to get here," Silverthorn said, his booming voice echoing against the walls of the castle.

Hope upon hope swelled within him. Evan smiled, and the warm sun on his face more than made up for the cool breeze that cut through his clothes and nearly into the core of him. The tip of his nose was cold and had lost all feeling, but he knew the men around him were far worse off.

"Bless you Silverthorn, and the one who sent you," Evan said.

"Your father gives his regards," Silverthorn said, and Evan wiped the corners of his eyes. Giddiness ran along the men, and conversations broke out.

The gate took more effort to open than Evan originally thought. The braces were easy enough to move, but the remains of the battering ram had to be pulled out and it had bent the portcullis terribly.

When they had opened the inner doors, and not without a fight and the sweat of many men, they were left with a gate that wouldn't raise more than a few feet before it was stuck at the top.

"May I suggest a solution?" Bill asked as Evan and Sam stood looking at the conundrum.

"Please," Evan said.

"Force bent it, perhaps force can bend it back?" A few of the thick, iron bars were almost broken, and one had snapped clean through and through.

"Dale," Sam said, then turned to a few men waiting. "Go get him and his hammers."

A few moments later the blacksmith had appeared. They had lowered the portcullis back into place, and the newly arrived soldiers were milling about.

A quick explanation of the situation was in order, and after that Dale examined the gate.

"I built it, I can put it back aright." He scratched his beard. "It won't be easy though. Give me a few minutes and I'll figure it out. Issac, give me the big hammer."

While he thought and prepared, Evan met Silverthorn off to one side, clasping hands through the portcullis.

"It's good to see you. It's good to see all of you." Evan was grinning from ear to ear. "Please tell me you brought food."

"More than enough to keep you fed until next year." Silverthorn nodded back toward the wagons. "And once we get it inside, we can enjoy some of it."

"I'm afraid it can't wait, and we need something to cook it with. We've been without firewood for a few days now." Evan wasn't sure why he didn't tell him the truth, that they had been cutting off pieces of the castle keep to burn for fuel for weeks, but it slipped out so smoothly it surprised him.

Silverthorn gave the order and food was brought to the portcullis. While Dale hammered at the bars in strategic places, the sound deafening in the small tunnel, they passed food through the bars. Men were dispatched to the forests to bring back firewood and the crack of a tree falling sounded beautiful.

It took them longer to get the tree cut up and transported back. By the time they had, Dale had beaten the portcullis into enough shape to raise it enough for men to come through crouched over.

Everyone was out in the courtyard, eyes gleaming and bright, laughter and shouting in the air. The mood was ecstatic. After such a long, hard winter Evan couldn't blame them.

Food wasn't the only thing Silverthorn had brought. Clothes, coats, and shoes were passed out. Thin hands clutched at them, pulled them under the gate, and wrapped them around thin frames.

Silverthorn watched them, a curious expression on his face.

"What is it?" Evan asked, after they were far enough from the others.

"They look too weak to have made it."

Evan felt a pang remembering those who didn't. Including the young boy, there were at least twenty in all. "We all made it, somehow." He stared off into the distance, until Silverthorn touched his elbow.

"Sorry, I lost myself."

The old captain scrutinized him with a searching look. "You've changed, my boy. No longer a boy, I see."

"No. No longer a boy." For all the desires he had of growing up, now that it had happened...

"Your father will hear the report. He will be pleased to hear that you all did so well."

Evan snorted. "Father pleased? Doubtful."

"Ah, you give him too little credit. The Archduke is a generous man, and he watches more than you think."

"Generous with a sharp tongue and a hard word." Evan looked down and ground the back of his boot into the rock hard soil. It had started to melt at the top, warmed by the sun and the constant tramping of boots. The white snow had turned a dirty brown now. "I don't want to talk about him though. What news of the King and his fighting? The last we heard there were raiders in the east giving him trouble."

Silverthorn looked like he was going to say something else about his father, but then reconsidered it and arched an eyebrow. "He's raised the armies and called the banner-men to him. They marched last year and were caught at the river crossing in an ambush." Silverthorn shook his head. "It was all they could do to keep from drowning in the river."

A chill ran down his spine. "You bring us ill news in difficult times."

"I can't help that it happened. Your father is with the King now, and most of his forces."

"He...wasn't in the battle, was he?" They continued offloading supplies, a barrel of cheese and butter was opened and spread among them. The carts were emptied now, barrels rolled under the opening and a long line of supplies waiting to get by. The first of the men who had gone into the forest were coming back across the plains, dragging corpses of trees to be cut up and burned.

"He was, and survived. Kept the left flank from collapsing and kept the retreat orderly. They set up on the bank in a defensive position, picketing as far as they could against surprise attacks." Silverthorn shook his head. "What a time for the Belmarch to regroup and come back."

"This was an advance party," Evan said. He licked his lips and eyed the cheese. The defenders were gorging themselves on it. Silverthorn motioned and one of his men brought some over. Evan took it and thanked him. "Who knows what they mean to do."

The first bite flooded his mouth with flavor, soaking in saliva and going down like butter. Evan devoured it as they looked on.

"Careful not to eat too much too fast. In your condition it will upset the stomach." Silverthorn motioned over to his sergeant. "Slow them down, will you? Order them."

The soldiers sprang into action, restoring order among the crowd that had gathered and was pressing in, hands reaching for food. It took a few minutes before order was restored. The soldiers got the starving defenders into a line and passed out food.

It was the smell that had brought them, and not just of the cheese and butter. There was meat, raw and salted, and biscuits and hard tack, and raw ingredients from the southern lands of Chathem. Silverthorn confided in him that there were even raisins, a present his mother had slipped in.

His mother thinking of him once again. They had been his favorite as a child, a delicacy that others couldn't afford.

And a reminder of what he had that others didn't. His thoughts must have shown through to his face, because Silverthorn dropped his voice and spoke in his ear.

"What bothers you?"

Evan realized the corners of his mouth had pulled down into a frown. He still had a block of cheese in his hand half eaten the rest of it a solid form in his stomach.

"How is my mother?" he asked, words stilted and too formal.

"The Archduchess is well, although she has been fraught with worry these past few months. After we lost contact with you…" Silverthorn shrugged. "You can thank her for convincing your father to send us, through correspondence of course. With the Archduke away she's had to bear the burden-" he cut off.

"That should have fallen to me." Evan held the cheese in his hand. He knew if he took another bite it would taste like ash.

"That's not what I meant," Silverthorn said, almost seeming flustered. His iron face had a tinge to it.

"I haven't been a good son, and I've been an even poorer duke." Evan held up a hand to stop Silverthorn from protesting. "I know what I was like, but now I have something else to live for, a purpose that I have been avoiding all my life. It falls to me to lead these people, and I intend to follow through with it."

Silverthorn said nothing, but watched him with pressed lips. Men were cutting up the timber now, hacking off branches and stripping away the sticks. The young children were picking them up by the bundle-full, laughing and smiling and taking them up to the Keep to be fed into the fire.

"You have grown more than I ever expected," he said at last. The smell of fresh cut wood drifted with the cool breeze, blessedly soft compared to the harsh winds they'd had. "Is this Yand's doing?"

"In part. Captain Yand died a few months ago, killed in an attack we were able to repulse."

"I'm sorry to hear that. He was a good man and a good friend."

Evan looked to the north. "Yes, he was."

"You two were close. You have my condolences."

"Thank you. Another thing I'd rather not talk about." Silverthorn nodded.

"My men can take care of the rest of the supplies. Shall we go in and discuss other matters?"

Evan nodded. "How rude of me not to invite you. Please, come in and join me in my study." He was feeling better, if not a little lightheaded, and finished the rest of the cheese as they walked across the courtyard.

Silverthorn filled him in on the trip, how many men he had brought, and the plans to bring up more workers in the springtime to bolster the ranks.

A fire was crackling in the fireplace when they entered his study, and Barger was feeding it logs. He rose and bowed to the Duke, then continued his task.

"You were saying?" Evan asked.

Silverthorn looked at the servant pointedly.

"Tell me what you can, it's been a while since we've had some warmth in this room and I don't intend to stop him." Evan stamped the snow off his feet and took his seat, offering his other to the old captain. "Besides, he isn't too bad once you get to know him."

Silverthorn's eyes widened, and he stared at him. Seeing him in such shock, after knowing how much it had taken to do it, gave Evan some amount of pleasure.

"May I offer you some wine?" Evan asked. Silverthorn nodded, and Barger got up and poured a glass, handing it over, then went back to the fire which was by now crackling merrily along and finally filling the room full of heat, and a good bit of smoke along with it.

Silverthorn took and drank. The smoke stung Evan's eyes, but it felt so good to be warm he didn't care. He sunk into his chair and sighed, but kept his coat on.

"Are you not going to have wine as well?"

Evan opened one eye. "Not anymore."

The corner of Silverthorn's mouth twitched, but his hand went to the sword at his side. "What have you done with Duke Hornblood?"

8

PASSING OF A FRIEND

Martha was hard at work in the kitchens, which were alive and lively for once. It had been so long since the fire was crackling and roaring in the fireplace that it brought a wave of emotion in Sam that threatened to overwhelm him.

She bustled around the kitchen, giving direction and laying a hand where needed. The chatter of the women was muted, damped by sheer hunger and exhaustion, but still there, nonetheless.

And the smells, oh the smells! Sam bathed in it, luxuriated it in, drank it all in. The smell of meat cooking, and smoke. Bread, long forgotten, now tickled his nose with its wonderful fluffy smell.

"Sam Freeman," Martha said, stopping in front of him with her hands on her hips. "If you keep standing there getting in the way with that loopy look on your face, I'll remove you myself."

Sam almost blushed. "Just here to help. What do you need?"

She arched an eyebrow, but then pointed over to a pot. "You can help by filling that up for me."

Others crowded at the door, enticed by the smells of food. They were going to have a real feast tonight. Sam took the cold pot by the handles and lugged it out to the well.

The snow didn't feel as bad with shoes on his feet that kept out the worst of the cold, and the new coat he got kept him mostly warm.

They had extras, the Hornblood supply train was expecting over a hundred defenders and twice as many family members, but the winter had taken its toll and starvation had claimed its victims.

Three bodies were hauled from the mass in the great hall once they were emptied out. Ned had been one of them.

Sam had kept that thought as far away from himself as he could, but his path took him by the bodies, and he couldn't help but look at him.

Cold and blue, devoid of the charm and life that had once filled him, Ned lay with the others in the snow. The other two were on top, not covered in snow like the rest that had died earlier.

There were too many of them. His heart wrenched, and he kept going with his full pot of water, trying to concentrate on it enough not to spill it.

Instead of thinking of those cold, lifeless eyes, Sam looked to the sky where the smoke from the fires inside the Keep rose. Three distinct plumes, one from the kitchen, one in the great hall, and one in the Duke's quarters, were swept away in the brisk winter breeze.

Clouds were coming behind it, another threat of snow-storm that lingered in the pale, blue sky.

Let it come. They were prepared now, able to access the forest for fuel that would burn away the worst of the cold.

It was good to get into the Keep and out of the elements, and the door slamming shut was a welcome tune since he was on the other side of it.

Laughter and voices drifted from the great hall, and Sam glimpsed them as he walked by. The Hornblood troops were arrayed along the tables, separated from the workers who were too tired to help or were eating to regain their strength.

Silverthorn was in the place of honor. Sam had seen him in action and approved of the man. He led his troops with discipline and sharp eye, not letting them get away with anything and keeping order with a soft word.

It was, Sam felt, a relief beyond measure. Of a quality of Captain Yand, Captain Silverthorn would relieve him of his burden and prove a good leader and adviser to the Duke.

Then, he was gone, back into the raging kitchens, and sought out Martha.

"Put it there." She had somehow re-acquired a spoon. Sam looked closer at it. It looked like the same one she always had in the kitchen, and she wielded it like a sword, smacking hands and fingers that tried to sneak and disrupt.

Careful not to spill, Sam put it on the hook by the fire. Martha swung it over, near enough to be licked by the three foot high flames that burned like beacons. "Now off with you," she said, shooing him away like a fly.

Did I detect a hint of a smile? An unruly lock of hair covered her eye. He fought the urge to push it away and listened to her direction.

The woman was confusing, and set his heart a-flutter. He was too old to be feeling this way, too far past his prime to prance and romp like a young stallion.

And yet, he held his head high as he walked out, aware of the glances and giggles of the other girls as he left.

Sam wasn't sure what to do now. He could wait for the cooked food or eat some of the dry rations they had out. He wasn't sure how long it would take to be ready, and he had filled up enough to beat back most of the painful hunger in his belly already.

A hint of guilt pulled at him, and he knew where he had to go.

Adjusting his coat, he marched past the great hall and back out into the cold of the courtyard.

A blast of cold air greeted him, and he turned back to the dead, stopping in front of Ned's rigid body.

Sam felt numb. He hadn't believed that Ned was dead, not really. Even now he thought those eyes would open under the bushy brows and give him a wink.

But that was not to be, and he knew it. Sam knelt down next to his friend. He was at a loss, unable to do anything and choked up.

Should I say something?

He reached out and touched Ned's hand. It was ice cold and felt like stone. He shrank back from it, unable to keep from shivering.

Would this be his fate too? Would he lay cold and dead?

The Keep was even less finished than it had been before the siege started, parts of it demolished to burn for the cook fires. From the day he had arrived it had been in a perpetual state of incompletion.

Will I leave it unfinished?

The thought of it scared him the most. Just another thing destroyed in his life, or left unfinished.

He hadn't promised he would finish it.

He slipped into memories. Meeting Ned for the first time, times of laughter, times of sorrow. How the man had imparted his wisdom.

It was all such a waste. A good man lay dead before him, his entire life gone in an instant, all so that someone else could steal, and take, and plunder something that didn't belong to them.

"Take care of them." He remembered the words on the wall, the promise that Ned made him make.

How he wished that he could go back and take those words back. They were a curse, spoken by his own mouth.

He sat and longed for the days of sweat and heat, for the time of building and creations and not destruction and death. He wished to go back, to keep on working, shaving after shaving, plank after plank.

But it was not meant to be. He realized that he mourned for that dead time almost as much as Ned, and it brought great shame upon him.

Sam hung his head. Ned lay cold and lifeless before him, and he couldn't take it anymore. There was no time to bury him, no way to break the earth as hard as rock, just like all the others.

"Perhaps it's a time to build then," Sam said. He released Ned, let him go off into the afterlife, and rose. Another grave, another death in a long line of them.

A loud cheer from inside the Keep distracted him. *They must have served the food.*

His mouth was watering, and the smell of food mingled with the smoke from the Keep. Sam turned, gave one last look at his dear friend, and went inside.

The feast was in full swing, and a great cloud of humidity rolled out of the doors as he entered. Sam breathed deep and licked his lips. His stomach grumbled watching the food platters run round the room passed from hand to hand.

There were heaps of it, more than he had seen being cooked, and the most that the hall had ever seen.

But it was Martha who captured his attention.

She directed the food, standing over the doors to the kitchen with her spoon as a scepter and a cudgel, a trained eye on all that surrounded her.

She still looked tired, and starved, but some food had brought color to her cheeks again, a hearty rose red.

It gave him some measure of joy to see. He wanted to talk to her, to understand how she was feeling, but there were so many people around he didn't think he would get the chance.

She looked at him then, and their eyes met. A quick glance away, and her eyes were back on his. *Did they linger?*

"Sam, pull up a seat and join us," Bill said, coming up behind him and clapping him on the back. Sam's gaze was broken, and when he looked back Martha had moved on.

He was torn for a second, wanting to go back to the other carpenters and sit with them, but with Ned being going he was left with Kerien and Trent, who looked like they were having a good time, but something didn't sit right with him. Would they accept him now that there was no Ned to soothe over the wrinkles in their relationship?

So, Sam turned and went with Bill, who was holding a big mug of ale, a ruddy complexion in his cheeks. He looked so merry and happy though that the twinge of apprehension boiled away within Sam.

The masons made up the bulk of the seating, and Bill took his place at the head of the table, but ordered room made for Sam. He put Sam at his right hand, shifting Barry down a seat. Sam gave him a glance, remembering the beating he had helped enact, but Barry didn't seem to remember, or didn't look like he harbored any ill will.

Plates heaped with food were passed around, carried out of the kitchen like treasure chests. A large deer, set on a spit, carried by the Duke's own servants, came out as the crowning piece, tender and steaming and giving off waves of a delicious aroma.

Then, the Duke arrived, Captain Silverthorn at his right hand. The conversation died down and the laughter stilled as he stood just inside the doorway.

His eyes flashed around the room. Sam hadn't expected him to come out, that he would be locked away within his tower.

Screams echoed in the dank, dingy tunnel. Raltone frowned at a drip of water from the ceiling, taking care to step well around it. "When they die make sure you keep their heads for display. Put them in a prominent position, but well below the Salz men. I wouldn't want the wrong message sent to the men."

"Yes, mi'lord," the gaoler mumbled. His face was so round and misshapen Raltone was surprised he was able to talk, but the strange accent that came with it made it almost impossible to tell.

Still, he was a master at what he did, and talking wasn't the reason he kept him around.

Sable walked behind him in the small corridor, following him up the winding halls and steep staircases back into the castle proper.

"The army is ready, we can move as soon as you give the order," he said.

"I know that isn't the reason you're here." Raltone gestured to his right as they emerged back into the ground floor. A servant ran over to brush off his boots, taking care to get every hint of dirt and mud. "You have something to ask, I presume?"

"Let me lead the army." Sable looked pale, deflated even. He still hadn't recovered from his previous experience. Neither, as Raltone had found out, had the other men. Those that had survived, that is. "I'll sweep through Chathem like a driving wind and reclaim the glory of the Belmarch."

It was slightly chilly in the hall as they entered, and Raltone snapped. A servant appeared, wrapping him with a cloak. Raltone sniffed. "Stoke the fires."

The new throne was ready, and Raltone gazed at it, ignoring Sable and the other men who gathered around. Vultures, every one of them. They wanted him dead, would pick at his corpse the moment they could.

They would take his hard work and shatter it. He wouldn't allow it though.

"You will command," he said, turning back to Sable, well within hearing of the others. This would travel faster than the winter wind that howled outside, the blasted weather that kept him pinned here in his seat of power.

Sable smiled, knowing that he was trapped. Raltone had spoken in public, quite clearly.

But the trap had been laid, and Raltone took his seat, admiring the plush arms and the comfortable cushion of it. The back, however, was so straight it almost leaned forward, a constant reminder of how fragile his hold on power was.

"But," he said, holding up a finger. "It will be a joint command. You will command half the forces, and General Granb will command the other half."

The smile was wiped out in an instant, but it was replaced. Raltone detested the young man, unable to hide his own emotions. A fool, but a useful tool to keep Granb in check.

"We move as soon as the passes are open. Prepare your men well." Raltone waved his hand. "Dismissed."

Sable bowed, spun stiffly, and marched off.

"And Sable." The man stopped and turned. "Don't fail me." Sable walked off, a hint of fear in his step.

Raltone leaned back, bumping into the throne. Chathem would fall, after so many years of effort by his predecessor, it would fall to him.

9

FEAST OF THE LONG WINTER

"To the men who came bearing gifts and life." The Duke raised his glass high into the air, then drank to their health. The toast was repeated, then the sound of a great cheer echoed through the hall. Backs were slapped, men were embraced, and the Duke slipped through the crowd to take the place of honor at the head table.

Sam watched him nimbly avoid notice. He looked so young but had grown up so much in the past few weeks. *How old is he, I wonder?*

Bill turned and whispered in his ear. "Looks like the Duke is back in the good graces of his subjects."

Sam turned back to see a sly grin on his face. "What are you planning?"

"Not a thing." Bill's look turned into one of complete innocence. Sam knew there was more, but he didn't care, and he didn't want to be swept up in it.

Despite the food and drink, he wished to be outside, back among the forest. He imagined himself there for a moment, running hands across bark, selecting the best trees to be felled. The cold breath of the winter still on his neck.

And then he was swept away, pulled into the rejoicing and merriment of the night. The ale and wine flowed, and the food seemed endless.

Sam found himself sneaking glances over at Martha through the night. The warmth of the kitchens had touched her face, giving it a warm glow, and the food had banished the worst of the darkness that had overtaken her. She was still a long way from healthy, but she didn't look so close to death now.

One of the younger girls swept up to her and placed a sprig of holly in her hair. Martha blushed and tried to take it out, casting a furtive glance in his direction, but the girl put it back in and scolded her.

The interaction, and the funny feeling in his stomach, made him reach for his ale, taking a deep draught of it. He imagined taking it out of her hair, brushing it back behind her ear, and kissing her.

He knew he shouldn't think of that, and he squeezed his eyes shut, draining the entire mug. Another was in his hands seconds later. There was an underlying sense of fear, one of dread, that this was not everything it seemed to be. Silverthorn laughed and drank with the rest of them, more grim than others, but joyful nonetheless.

What would it be like to let him take control, to lead the training sessions with the tradesmen who weren't cut out to be soldiers? He imagined that now that there was a professional fighting force he would no longer be needed.

Then he glanced at his side. Bill was leading the conversation surrounding him, so intent upon himself he didn't notice Sam watching. Was this in Bill's best interest, now that there were others with more power in the castle?

It all made his head hurt, and then another glance at Martha made it all the worse. He didn't know what to think about her, but deep down he knew that she was off limits. It wouldn't be right to her dead husband, a good man taken by sickness and tragedy to swoop in and steal her from his memory.

Or was that even a possibility? Was that something he was just pretending to want, that he thought about to make himself feel better?

As far as he knew Martha didn't like him much, if at all, let alone love him.

Love.

Thinking the word made him squishy inside. It was too much to commit to, too dangerous of a concept. After all, wasn't he the one who had killed and murdered less than a few months ago? What kind of man like that deserved love, let alone the love of a kind and generous woman like Martha.

Someone bumped into him, spilling his drink all over the table. The group surrounding him roared with laughter.

Sam didn't find it funny, licking the liquid off his lips and trying to find something to wipe his dripping face off.

"Here, drink up," Bill said, pushing another mug of beer into his hand. Someone else threw him a small towel, and he used it to mop himself off.

"I shouldn't have anymore." It was going to his head, which was already lightheaded, but it did have a relaxing effect on his muscles.

"Come on, what will it hurt? This is a day to remember, let's make the night to match." Bill grinned at him, like a coyote over a rabbit.

"You're right. I should lighten my load a little." He took what looked like a long pull, but was only just a small amount out of the mug. Whoever had poured it had left little head on it, but it still got into his nose and tickled.

"Lighten your load, and loosen that belt." Bill slapped him on the stomach, almost making him spit out his ale. Sam glared at him, but he had moved on already, telling a bawdy tale to his drinking companion next to him.

It devolved into something that made his ears burn, and he wanted to curl up and leave, but instead he contented himself to turn to the mason next to him, Barry.

"Pass me the bread, will you?" Sam held out his hand, and he handed it over.

"What's got into your pants tonight?" Barry squinted with one eye. "Not grateful enough to the others around us? Seems to me there's plenty of reason to be happy."

There was something about the tone in the older man's voice that set him on edge, and put his teeth together in a clench. Sam still remembered the night in Bill's cabin and hadn't forgiven him for it.

Not that they had asked forgiveness anyway.

"I'll get my strength back and then feel grateful." Sam bit into the bread, warm and delightful. It had cooled some, but was almost fresh out of the ovens.

"You'll get more than strength back if you keep this up." Barry leaned in closer and leered at him. "She's been watching you all night. A little more ale might bring her to your bed for a rough and tumble."

Anger rose in him, at his bad breath, at his crude language, and what he could only assume was directed at Martha. Sam breathed through his nose, trying to contain himself, but Barry continued.

"What? Not interested? That's fine by me, give me a few minutes alone with her and I'll be the one enjoying myself." He laughed crudely. "Saggy tits and all."

Sam felt the thing locked away stir, but he couldn't help it.

It purred, slinked around his mind, and he felt his vision haze over. It wasn't just the alcohol, although that was catching up to him now too, it was more than that.

And then he saw Martha, hazarding a glance in her direction. She wasn't looking at him, caught in a conversation with the girl next to her, but she was chatting away.

All he had to do was walk away, or tell a quick joke to diffuse the situation. He thought of one, flashing through his mind, but out of rage and spite he discarded it.

This may be a night of celebration, but the man had gone too far.

Sam stood and turned to him. He didn't know what he was supposed to do, but he reached out and poured his ale over his head.

Barry fell back, sputtering and spitting curses at him, then banged his head on the ground. Others were up around him in an instant, surrounding him.

All Bill's men.

Sam threw down the mug, and the handle broke as it hit the stone floor with a clatter. The laughter in the room continued, but there was talking and whispering near him.

"I'll kill you for that," Barry said, wiping his face and rising.

Bill was in between them, before Sam could even take a step forward. He didn't say a thing, but fixed his eye on Barry.

"Get him out of here," Bill said. "What's gotten into you?" he shouted at the retreating man. "Treat Sam with the respect he's owed."

But Sam's rage had not died down, and a simple act such as that wasn't going to satisfy the thing inside him.

This is why I'll never create, why I'll never finish.

"Talk to me Sam." Bill was in his face, and Sam blinked. The room had gone quiet now, and everyone was staring at him.

Martha and the Duke included.

Sam licked his lips, tasting the remnants of the ale. *What was I thinking?*

With so many eyes on him, he was able to suppress the thing and drain the rage inside him, replacing it with a heavy dose of shame.

"Just a tumble, that's all," Sam mumbled, feigning drunkenness. "I must have had too much to drink."

"That's so." Bill turned to the crowd. "We've all had a little too much to drink tonight, haven't we? I'll drink to that!" He raised his own mug and downed it in a few seconds, then raised it high.

The masons cheered, shattering the tense air that had pervaded the room, and the cheers spread to the others. The ale kept flowing, and mugs were drained, but Sam didn't know what to do.

He sat back down, easing off his wobbly legs. All of his energy had deflated, leaving him feeling empty and lightheaded.

"Why did you do that to me?" Sam asked.

Bill turned his chair to Sam, sitting beside him. "Whatever do you mean?"

"You know. Don't play dumb with me now."

"I haven't done a thing, Sam. I'm sorry that you have lingering resentment to Barry." There was more than a hint of danger in Bill's eyes. "As for me, what's happened in the past between us is all water under the bridge as far as I'm concerned."

"Water under the bridge?" Sam echoed, then shook his head. It was clearing, and he was regaining his focus. Every fiber in his being wanted to look at Martha, but he resisted.

Instead, he looked up toward the head table. The Duke was watching him, and they locked eyes. What was going on behind them, Sam couldn't tell, but it wasn't joy or mirth.

It was altogether something different.

"I don't want to play these games," Sam said, rising again sharply. "You can if you want, but I refuse. Now, I still have a job to do and a castle to finish, which I intend to do, so if you don't want to help me then you keep out of my way."

His voice was raised, and he knew it, but he couldn't help it, the words seemed to flow from him in his exhausted and drained state. Sam had eaten all he really needed anyway, and he avoided the sudden stares and sharp eyes that watched him as he turned and walked away.

"No, let him go," Bill said as he walked away, probably to one of his henchmen.

With friends like that I'd rather take the Belmarch. He stomped out into the cold of the courtyard, looking up into the sky and wrapping his hands around himself. Stars twinkled in the clear sky, and the moon hung in a half round lower on the eastern horizon.

Sentries patrolled the wall, actually walking where before they had not enough strength to move, but every now and then one of them cast a look in the direction of the Keep. Sam didn't blame them. The sounds of joy and laughter drifted out of it.

As his body cooled his head cleared. The anger dissipated into the cold night air and the thing coiled deep inside him went back to sleep. He urged it there, calmed it where it had been riled up, and was grateful that he hadn't gone too far.

He was within a breath of stabbing the man with the knife that lay gleaming on the table beside his plate. He wondered if that wasn't the point of Bill inviting him to eat there.

Sam shivered. He knew he couldn't stay out much longer, but he didn't want to go back inside and face the others. *I couldn't control myself.*

Before he turned to go back in, he cast one last look up into the sky. One day he would be free of the shackles that bound him, that forced him into a life he hated.

One day he would be free to build and not tear down. To create and not destroy. "One day I will be free," he whispered.

10

OLD WOUNDS

Evan watched Sam leave the great hall with interest. He moved like a fighter, unable to mask it in the pure emotion that overtook him. The Duke glanced back at Bill, who seemed pleased with himself.

What game is he playing?

"Who is that man?" Silverthorn asked, keeping his voice low enough so that only Evan could hear it.

"The master carpenter, Sam Freeman." Evan took up his goblet, filled with pure water. The smell of wine and ale tempted him. He wanted to taste it, to drain the cups of it until it poured out oblivion into his soul.

But he had duties and obligations tonight and would for the rest of his life.

Conversation returned to the room, which had fallen in a hush. The newcomers made mention of the incident, the mason that had been humiliated now dusted off and been sent off to bed with by few of his companions.

"And what do you think of him, Silverthorn?" Evan asked, poking at the meat on his plate. "Given your... short amount of time that you have known of him."

"A dangerous man." Silverthorn looked at the door. "But he seems to garner respect among these men."

Evan smiled and recounted the stories that had been told to him. The beating back of the attacks, the slaying of the giant.

He left out the part about him crafting the crest above his desk. He wasn't sure why, other than it seemed a trivial matter.

"And what do you think of him, Your Highness?"

Evan considered the question and rested his head on his hand. *What do I think of him?*

He was conflicted. By what, Evan didn't know, but he had seen others in the same way, sometimes himself.

"There is more to him than meets the eye," he said at last.

"A bland and trite response. That is the Duke that I know." Silverthorn took a sip from his goblet, ignoring the scowl that Evan shot his way.

"You better still have the ear of my father, otherwise I'd have you punished for that."

"Your father pays me to tell him the truth, and I'm not about to stop for some snot nosed son of his who can't bear it." The last Evan knew as an intentional tweak, pushing him to do something he would regret.

"I regret to inform you that I've grown up past those immature ways," Evan said. "Now I find myself in charge of an entire castle's worth of defenders and their families. You won't get the rise out of me that you used to Silverthorn."

Silverthorn matched his gaze with one that was more steely and filled with danger. Evan was more than a little scared of the man and had been since he was younger. "Besides, it wouldn't be right to beat the old." Evan let the insult slip out smoothly.

It lodged deep, only the slightest narrowing of Silverthorn's eyes giving him away, but give him away it did.

Finally, after what seemed like an eternity locking eyes, a half-smile crept up the edge of his face. "You have grown up."

"Not as much as you think."

Silverthorn laughed then, a big, hearty laugh that drew Evan in and forced him to join in.

It felt good. He couldn't even remember the last time he had laughed so well or so long, and his insides started to ache because of it.

But, eventually, the laughter died down. Silverthorn clapped him on the shoulder and lifted his glass.

"I drink to you, Your Highness, and the man you have yet to become."

"And I drink to you, and the man you once were." Evan winked at him, and, exchanging grins, they both drank up from their cups.

The rest of the night passed quickly, the merriment and happiness unleashed from months of hardship all the more pronounced. Soon couples were retiring to nooks and crannies of the castle, openly displaying their intentions to those around.

Not everyone had a family though, and Evan could sense the divide that opened between those with families and those without. Jealous, alcohol induced glances were shot at the pairs as they tripped and wobbled through the doorway.

"Give them some time," Silverthorn said, when he noticed Evan watching. "The night is young, and the times are evil."

"They aren't the ones I'm worried about." Evan chewed on his lip, and clasped his empty cup tight. "Not that I'm not jealous of them, I could use the arm of a good woman around me right now, but I don't know..." He struggled to find the right words without sounding petty, or childish.

"You have no women of the night to satiate the needs of the men," Silverthorn said.

"You always had a way with words, always dancing around what you wanted to say."

Silverthorn shrugged. "For all the time you've spent running around chasing my shadow and training with me I thought you would appreciate the bluntness."

Blunt was exactly what the man was. "A few days ago I was trying to think of ways to keep them alive." Evan looked around at the dwindling numbers still in the great hall. They were almost all drunk lingerers, without the strength to pull themselves back to their own beds, or men bedding down for the night.

A pair came back, looking disheveled. "Now they have other needs that I didn't even consider." A thought struck Evan, one that he hadn't even considered before then.

"How does my father manage it?"

Silverthorn drained his cup. "He's had a lot of practice, and he has progeny to think of. How he does it?" He shrugged. "That lies far above my realm and pay. But I suspect his father was hard on him too, always preparing him for what was to come."

Old wounds were coming back to the surface, and they stung. Evan wanted to push them away, but at the same time this was the first time he had Silverthorn's full and undivided attention. Few men knew his father better.

"You speak as if my father cares about me," Evan said roughly. He took up his knife and stabbed half a loaf of bread, bringing it to his lips and tearing off a chunk.

"Your father is the Archduke. He must be above reproach, show no favoritism. Or that's what he always told me." Silverthorn turned his chair, facing Evan.

"Did you know that he asked me to teach you, long before Yand?"

"You? He couldn't do that, he would be lost without you leading the guard." Evan was aghast at the very suggestion of it.

"Your mother was against it. She said I was too rough and would break you. Like a ship against the rocks, she said. So, deferring to your mother's wishes, he appointed Yand." Silverthorn watched him with a stone face. The room was quiet now, just a few whispers and murmurs and snores from the side of the room where the beds had been shoved up against the wall to make room for tables.

"I think now that they both were wise. From Yand you learned a great deal more than you would have from me, and it will serve you well far into the future."

"I don't believe you." Evan shook his head. He set the bread back down. He didn't feel like eating anymore, his stomach finally satisfied for the first time in weeks. "You've been one of Father's favorites ever since I've known you."

"Or I've known you." Silverthorn dipped his head.

"So why would he waste your talents and your loyalties on me?"

He didn't say anything for a while. Silverthorn had always been cautious, decisive when he did act, but cautious. Father said that's what made him such a good guard.

"That is a question only you and he can answer." Silverthorn stood and stretched, his joints creaking as he did. "If you'll excuse me, Your Highness, the road was long and the travel cold for a man of my age. It is far past time I should have retired."

Evan returned his bow, and the man walked away back to his room. The fire had died down in the great hearth, but a young girl was at it now adding logs. Each one she tossed made embers dance and fly, and Evan stared into the red, flickering glow.

His mind was a mess of questions and confusion, things he had thought he knew now cast in doubt. For so many years his father had been hard on him, abused him, was cold to him. How could he possibly have wanted what was best for him?

And yet, here he was sending one of his most trusted men north during war with the eastern raiders. By all accounts Silverthorn should have been right by his father's side and should have been.

Evan shook his head. No, it must have been that the fighting had died down for the season, that the raiders had retreated east like they always did and that there was another explanation for this.

And he thought he knew what it was.

The Archduke didn't trust him. He was still the young boy who didn't know his way around anything, and he needed looking after.

Silverthorn was here as a minder, as a spy. He was here to report on how Evan was faring and what other mistakes he had made, like usual.

His hand tightened around his cup, and he glanced over at one filled with wine. It would be so easy to reach out and take it.

That's what my father would expect me to do. To take the easy way out, drown myself in alcohol once again. Evan gnashed his teeth, railed against the feeling of desire that welled up inside him like a river about to overflow its banks.

But still, he wanted it. It would make all his problems go away, for a moment at least. Or, for a night.

Who would he be in the morning? And what would he feel? He knew.

Evan couldn't take it anymore, and pushed away from the table and almost ran out the door into the hall. A few more steps brought him out of the Keep and into the courtyard.

He took a deep breath of the cold, night air. It burned his lungs coming in, but he felt it and rejoiced. It was something different, at least, than to fall prey to the temptation that waited inside.

Despite the cold, he decided to go up to the walls and see how the men were doing. He wished they could have joined in, but they had been fed before they left, or had been relieved of their watch to join in for a few minutes or so, coming and going with the crowds.

Now, they walked on the walls, finally showing some sort of life. Evan shivered, but took care on the cold steps. They were icy and dangerous, liable to send a man over the edge to his death.

"Good evening, Your Highness," the sentry closest to him said upon seeing him emerge from below. He tipped his head and held a fist to his brow, open to show it was empty.

Evan greeted him and returned the salute. His breath made gusts of fog. "Have you seen anything unusual?"

The sentry smiled a sloppy grin, which surprised Evan. "Nothing outside the walls, if that's what you mean. There have been quite a few... couples taking their leave though."

Evan couldn't help but feel a sense of squeamishness. Not that he cared much, but there was something about the night that made everything seem like it had been held back for too long.

The castle was like a kettle boiling, and had been for some time, but tonight the steam was coming out. *I wonder how mine will show?*

"If they aren't too loud, let them have their fun," he finally said in response. He was getting too cold to stay up here, and the night breeze was chilling him through his clothes.

It was a reminder of what they had gone through, and Evan stared up to the north, as a reminder of what was going to come.

Evan bid the man good night, making his excuses, and turned. Something caught his eye, however, and he stopped.

It was a flash, or so he thought, somewhere far into the distance. *Near the tree line.*

"What is it, Your Highness?" the sentry stood at his side.

He peered into the dark. *The river was too high, too rough to try and cross this time of year. It couldn't possibly be the Belmarch, could it?*

But at the pit of his stomach, a lump of dread was spreading.

11

AT THE WALLS OF IRONWOOD

The days passed quickly on the road, and Rhys felt his strength returning with every meal. He didn't feel the need to gorge himself with food now, like it would be gone when he turned his head, and the travels even started to feel pleasant.

The weather was nice, the sky clear and sunny with a crisp chill to the air. The snow was fresh from the storm that had come in before they had left, and made for good sledding.

"We're making good time," Rhys remarked as they set off from their lunch time stop.

Poppy made a sign and spit into the snow, then mumbled underneath his breath.

"What was that?"

"You bring ill fortune speaking in that way."

Rhys was shocked. "What? Just by commenting on how well our progress was?"

Once again Poppy made his sign and spit. "There it is again. Don't you know you don't ask for sun when it's raining and ask for rain when it's sunny?"

"Why not? Wouldn't that make the most sense? You won't want or need rain if its already raining."

"You inlanders, always wanting and hoping for things. You should be grateful for living in the present, in the now." He took out his pipe and lit it with a quick strike of his tinderbox, then gave his horse a gentle flick.

The sled jerked forward, then slipped into cutting a groove in the snow. Rhys reflected on the words, not happy about being called an inlander.

"You have a point, but I'm not appreciative of how you said it."

Poppy gave a small chuckle, which inflamed Rhys even more. He knit his brows and sunk into the seat. "How long do you think we have until we get there?"

"Depends on the weather. A few days, maybe more." Poppy shrugged. "Or it could take weeks."

"Weeks? Surely you can't mean that?"

"If we get caught in a blizzard..." He clicked the pipe between his teeth. It was hand carved, with a fish on the bowl, and he wrapped his dark hand around it.

He let the matter drop and Rhys contented himself to watching as the landscape changed on their journey.

The farms continued, for what seemed like forever, until the flat lands started to hump and heave into rolling hills.

The journey was harder now, with the horse having to pull them uphill, but the lightening of their load by eating and burning helped.

Rhys retreated into himself, content to let Poppy smoke his pipe and lead the horse on with careful attention to the reins but only a light touch.

They passed into lands that Rhys was familiar with, stopping for the night in a farmer's barn to keep warm from the biting cold.

Meals were simple, but filling, and after a quick breakfast they were off once more.

To pass the time he worked through the list of people he should visit first, and who would be less likely to help.

His recent fall from grace had hurt his standing in the court, but Rhys thought that Tabitha might be his best bet. She still owed him for getting her out of that tight spot.

He chuckled to himself. She should have been more careful, or taken less lovers. One or two were easy enough to hide from her clueless husband, but five was a bit much.

"What is it?" Poppy was staring at him, smoke drifting from his pipe.

"Nothing."

"Laughing by yourself when no joke is told might be considered something where I'm from. I don't know what it means to you."

The sun was splashing a dazzling display of colors on the low clouds. Rhys caught a whiff of pine beneath the pungent odor of manure and horse.

"Palace intrigues, and a long forgotten memory." *Had it been that long?* He wracked his brain, trying to pinpoint when it was. Not more than a few years ago.

Poppy grunted. "Sorry I asked."

"Not in your boathouse?"

"Not even remotely." The man looked straight ahead, pipe firmly clamped between his teeth.

But Rhys was tiring of the long silences, and his regains strength had renewed him more than he thought. He couldn't bear to take more miles in quiet.

"What would you do, if you were in my place?" Rhys asked. He scratched his chin, hanging loosely and filled with stubble. How he wished for a warm bowl of water and a sharp razor again.

"I don't envy your task, not one bit."

"That doesn't answer my question." Rhys looked closer at him, searching his face for a tell. "Anyone with eyes can see you're well thought of in your village, and I'm guessing it wasn't by accident."

Poppy glanced over at him. "Are you asking for my advice?"

"I am."

He sniffed, then blew a smoke ring that was split apart and blown away by the wind almost as soon as it was out of his mouth. "Things have changed in the court, from what I have heard. The King is far more worried about the eastern raiders than the northern ones."

"The Belmarch are far more dangerous than the eastern raiders."

"That may be, but it has been years since the Belmarch posed any real threat to us. The raiders, on the other hand, have invaded once a year for the last decade."

"And then they leave. Everyone knows that they aren't here to stay, only to pillage and return."

"But they haven't."

Rhys sat upright. The implications of that one little sentence ran through his mind like lightning. "What do you mean they haven't?"

Poppy shrugged. "They've been staying for the last few years, getting a foothold. And the King has been having a tough time getting rid of them. One of his most troublesome problems, I'd say. The southern lords have been clamoring and complaining non-stop since it started."

"And so that's why we've been neglected for so long."

"It's hard to listen to a boy when the wolf's at your doorstep."

It all seemed to make sense now, the ignored pleas for help, the dwindling resources sent their way. It seemed like only the Hornbloods had been sending supplies north for the last few months before the siege and now Rhys suspected that was the case.

So why hadn't his sources told him? It set a troubling spike deep in his heart, and shook him to the very foundation of his being.

Things were far more grim for Chathem than he originally suspected, and Poppy seemed to sense his discomfort.

"It isn't all bad. The King has raised his armies and marched east, expelling them for the season. He's stationed a large garrison on the border of the Golden River, and I suspect the raiders will have a harder time getting across this time."

"How many years has this been happening?" Rhys asked quietly, secretly counting the time.

Poppy didn't say at first. The sled scraped over the snow, the old mare pulling quietly along. "Three years."

Just about a year into the castle's construction. And a few after his fall from grace.

"We'll stop for lunch in a few hours." Poppy squinted against the sun, watching its height up above. Clouds were gathering in the east, but it was calm and clear where they were.

For now.

There was a burden in the air, a heaviness that went into his bones and troubled him. Some of it was the weather, the rest...

Rhys wasn't feeling well, not well at all. Whatever would come of his journey, he wasn't sure that he could help Castle Hornblood now.

And that hurt him the most.

The promise he had made, the look in their eyes as he splashed into the river and broke away, the cheer going up on the castle walls.

It might all be for nothing.

Rhys swallowed, choking back his feelings. He wanted someone to yell at, to scream at, and berate.

But there was only him, Poppy, and an old mare in the rolling hills of Chathem.

So, all he could do was hold it in and hope that there was a miracle waiting in Ironwood.

Then, there it was. He saw it emerging from the hill as they crested it, a long way off but shining in the sun and the fresh snow brought the night before.

The great white walls of Whitehall glimmered, reflecting the sun from the snow like diamonds.

The road had been well traveled the last day of their journey, and the track trodden well. The road was straight now, leading to the Northern Gate set into the wide walls of Ironwood.

As they approached the guards on the wall were more visible, sentries set to watch for threats seemed so laughable this far into the center of Chathem, but Rhys knew how quickly those enemies could travel.

"Here we are," Poppy said. "I'll take you as far as Whitehall and no further."

"You don't have to do that, I can make my own way from here."

"Nonsense, I have business to attend to. I told you as much before we left."

Rhys murmured his thanks, grateful for not having to walk in the snow. The boots they had given him didn't fit quite well enough, and were too loose, but he wasn't going to complain in front of him.

Not after all their kindness.

In his heart was a big knot though, and a lump of dread resting in his belly. There were so many questions that he had to answer and had no good answer for them.

Whatever the case, he had to remember the defenders of the castle. They were relying on him to do his best.

But he wasn't sure it was going to be good enough.

The pit deep in his stomach wasn't going away. Rhys had hoped with the sighting it would, but it had only grown larger.

They joined a small caravan on their way to the gate, the road turned somewhat muddy. Poppy kept off the road and in the hard-packed snow and ice just off to the side.

The wind blew their direction, taking the smells of the city with it. Rhys wrinkled his nose at the smell of the filth layered into the smoke and baking bread. It sparked a familiar note though and brought up memories he wished had laid dormant.

They stopped in the line waiting at the gate. Traffic had slowed to a crawl as the guard questioned those entering the city.

"Why are they doing this?" Rhys asked. Poppy only shrugged. They seemed to be stopping every cart and traveler, uncharacteristically since the last time he had been in Ironwood.

Another troubling sign.

An old woman carrying a basket was next. The guards lifted the lid, peering inside. A few words were exchanged, and the woman passed into the city.

Men were watching from the battlements, spears in hand. Rhys noted the bows, strung and at the ready, and wondered what kind of fear had overtaken the city.

"Waste of time, wish they would hurry up," the man behind them said. He was carrying wood on his back, straining against the weight of it and crouched over. Rhys commiserated with him privately, then a thought struck him and he turned.

"Say, friend, it's been a while since I've been in the city. What's all the fuss about?"

The man looked at him with one lazy eye, the other staring off into the distance. "You haven't heard about the attack?"

A stab of concern struck him, but he kept it out of his voice. "Attack? No, not at all," Rhys said.

"Eastern raiders came up last harvest, went undetected through the border and all the way to the city." The old man sniffed, and the line moved forward as another was admitted into the city. "Scaled the walls in the middle of the night and made it to Whitehall. Almost killed the King, I hear, but he fought them off and killed them in his nightclothes."

"I didn't know." Rhys exchanged glances with Poppy. "No wonder they've increased the guard."

"Increased? The King is going to wage war on them when spring comes, take every fighting man he can, or so I hear."

"He's already called in the southern lords," a young woman said, breaking into the conversation. "Aunt Jamy said so last week when she was here."

"And the northern lords have pledged their troops too," her companion said, a much older middle aged woman. "He'll save us from them, make sure they can never do it again."

Rhys turned his attention back to the guards, they were next in line. "This doesn't look good," he whispered to Poppy.

"It doesn't look good for my sled either." He pointed to the road up ahead, a pile of mud instead of fresh snow. "I'm not sure I can get through."

Rhys looked up. The guards were staring at him, or behind him. He looked back, but he couldn't see anything of note.

A rough hand grabbed his shoulder and spun him around. An equally matched guardsman, with a chipped front tooth looked him up and down. He turned back and bellowed to the others "That's him, take him."

<h1 style="text-align:center">12</h1>

<h2 style="text-align:center">ALONE AGAIN</h2>

"You could stay longer." Evan watched Silverthorn packing, taking what little he had and returning it to his trunk. He had the biggest room besides Evan. It had belonged to Overseer Rhys when he was still here, but his rank had meant it was left open.

Now, Evan leaned against the door frame. A tweak in his memory made him stand up straight, the look of Yand from far ago and a simple rebuke of not standing up straight. *Even now he haunts me.*

"I must return. I have my orders and they are to go back as soon as everything is seen to here."

"But it isn't. You know that the Belmarch can return."

"They won't be here this winter, I can tell you that much. You couldn't move an army in snow like that, and it'll be worse north of the river."

Evan knew he had a good point, but he didn't want to be left on his own again. The man had just gotten here less than two weeks ago, and now he was set to leave.

Leaving him alone once again.

He had grown used to the conversations, of not having to hold himself back like he did among the others. It was... good to have someone closer to his own rank that he could talk with.

Of course, his father had ordered him back again.

"Levitus is a good man, and a good commander. He's a solid choice and will keep the men in line."

"He isn't a tactician, or a trainer like you. He doesn't know how to take the men and turn them into a fighting force." Evan chewed his lower lip. "And neither do I."

"I thought you trusted this man of yours, the carpenter." Silverthorn tucked the last of his clothes into the chest, then shut and locked it. He turned back to Evan to give him his full attention. The case smelled like horse leather and steel, things Evan had always associated with the guard. Now, he knew why.

"I had to. He was the only one with fighting experience. Father didn't send me his brightest and most experienced fighters, and the men the King supplied didn't know much either."

"It sounds like you're complaining, Your Highness." Silverthorn wore his iron mask, but the hint of disapproval was evident. *Still treating me like a child.*

"He's proven himself, but I don't think I can rely on him." Evan sighed and sat in the chair. Silverthorn motioned to the one across and Evan waved, giving him permission to sit.

"I can't tarry any longer."

"Even though the roads are snowed in and hard to travel?"

"Even so. More-so. I have to get back to your father. You're Duke Hornblood and bear the title and his blood. You will do fine here, and you will hold the castle."

"With what forces? A few dozen more men?" Evan shook his head.

"You survived a siege." Silverthorn shrugged. "I will speak to your father, give him a message."

"What good will that do? He has no time for me."

"He set you in this place, a place of honor and one of challenge."

"Honor?" The word rang cold against the rough stone walls. A fire crackled in the fireplace, keeping back the worst of the cold, but the walls were leaky and drafty. "What honor is it to stand here in the north, in an unfinished castle, and with not enough men to hold it?"

"Your Highness, you were given one hundred men."

"Ninety-nine," Evan interrupted.

"Myself not included, more than enough to keep an invading army at bay. You have archers aplenty, and with enough arms to keep you supplied in the event of an attack. But yes, your father considers this duty one of honor."

The anger that was creeping in while Silverthorn was talking had burned in his insides for years. A hatred, on the verge of love, that he didn't know existed.

It made him want to drink, and drown the anger in a flood of wine or ale.

Instead, Evan took a deep breath, trying to restore himself. It wasn't working.

"Then a message to him I will send." Evan tried to keep the bite out of his voice. He wasn't sure he succeeded, but Silverthorn showed no emotion in his face. He bent his head in a bow of acknowledgment.

Evan worked his jaw, holding back the worst of his words. He stood and paced around the small room. "Send this message to him. Father, it is your son. I have held the castle despite the winter and a siege by the Belmarch. They intend to send more than what they tried to take us with when the weather clears. I will try my best to reinforce the defenses but am lacking in men to build as I have lost over half my working men to hunger and cold.

"Your son will stand alone in the north, and he will live or die trying to fulfill his duty." Evan bit back an insult that he wanted to hurl, wondering if Silverthorn would faithfully reproduce it word for word or if he would blunt the anger and the hatred that leaked through. "I expect nothing more from you than what you have already provided. I may live to see you again. With deepest regards Duke Evan Hornblood."

"Are you sure you don't want to write that down?" Silverthorn asked.

"I don't have anything to write with," Evan lied.

Silverthorn got up, moving to his chest, but Evan stopped him. "I wouldn't trust myself to keep a civil hand if I did."

"As Your Highness wishes."

The anger had fizzled somewhat but was still a cold ember. Silverthorn threw another log on the fire. It spit and hissed, still green from being freshly cut.

"I'll take lunch and then set off."

Evan didn't have the heart to argue, but he wanted him to stay. Once again, he would find himself alone in the world, no familiar faces to keep him company and talk to. Just a group of soldiers and builders, and no real way to control them.

On the other hand, with the reinforcement of his own men Evan was now more secure that the castle wouldn't rise up against him and kill him.

They ate in Silverthorn's room, waited on by Barger and the rest of the servants. Evan ate it and conversed politely, but it felt like sand in his mouth with no flavor at all.

All too soon Silverthorn was dressed and ready, his chest loaded up on the cart with his small entourage of two other men at his side.

He was here less than a month, and the winds were getting warmer. A few more months would see spring start to come through, and the snow would melt.

Evan felt it was bittersweet, finally seeing an end to the worst of the weather, but now he would face the threat of an invasion head on.

And they couldn't stop an army with a hundred men.

"Your Highness. You will do fine here, don't fear." Silverthorn reached out a mailed hand and grabbed onto his shoulder. "I will do what I can, and inform your father of the situation. I know there will be more help on the way."

"Travel safely Captain Silverthorn." Evan embraced the man, his strength nearly crushing him. *Oh, to have him at my side in a fight. What I wouldn't give to have an army of him.*

Then he was on his horse. With a final salute Silverthorn clicked his heels and set out. The horse turned and rode, with the cart trundling behind him.

Evan felt worse than he ever had, and more alone than he had since he learned of Yand's death. The small band of men passed through the open gates and into the road beyond the castle, stopping the line of men bringing felled trees and stone into the courtyard.

The sounds of hammers rang around the courtyard once again. Evan wasn't sure if it was the blacksmith or the masons, but it had been a long time since he had heard that. He didn't want Silverthorn to go, not just because he was a competent soldier and capable leader, but he knew there was something more to it.

So, he crossed the yard and ascended the wall, watching them disappear into the woods with an ache in his heart.

Perhaps it is because he is the only connection I had to my family. He didn't like thinking of it, but he knew it was probably true. How was he supposed to bear his family name and do well of it, when he had so little skill and experience to speak of?

As he stood on the wall, feeling the cold wind on his body, Evan cursed his past self. Always shirking responsibility, always trying to get out of everything just so he could feel better about himself.

The drinking, the carousing, the foolish play. It was all an attempt to escape something bigger, something stronger than himself.

And the desire to drink came back upon him in force. It burned in his throat, itched his lips. Evan licked them, feeling his mouth go dry.

A little drink would cure it, bring back the moisture he needed. And it would drown out the problems that seemed to keep piling up. It would be a way out, and a way out was what he needed right now.

"Everything in order, Your Highness?" Sam asked, from behind him.

Evan hadn't heard him come up behind him but turned now. "Fine. How are the carpentry supplies?" he asked awkwardly.

"The Belmarch burned the best of it while they were here." Sam spat the words out, then realized how he sounded. "No offense by my tone."

"None taken. You are a foreigner, are you not?"

"I am."

"Where do you come from?"

Sam shifted. "I'd prefer not to answer, if you don't mind."

Bold. A small hint of anger came up inside him, but Evan stifled it. What right did he have to demand anything of him?

But he was still the Duke of Hornblood, and he could not tolerate this. He had to do something. His father would have had the man whipped for insubordination, but he wasn't sure that would work.

And he wasn't sure who would do the whipping.

Evan frowned. "I should have you punished for that."

"Go ahead." Sam didn't even bat an eye. He seemed to know what kind of predicament Evan was in. Or, he didn't care. "While we're fighting among ourselves there are others out there who would gladly come and slit our throats."

"You think they'll be back?" Evan didn't know why he asked it. He knew the answer.

So did Sam, but he turned back to the courtyard instead. "I need your blessing to build what I had in mind before, with some changes."

"What kind of changes?"

"Dangerous changes." His face was tight, lips spread into a fine line. Age was showing at his temples, graying that once before had been brown. "And ones that will make more work for the masons."

"So, this is what it is about." Evan crossed his arms. The man hadn't even given him a few moments peace by himself before coming with his demands.

He had seen it done many times before but had never been the one taking the full brunt of it. He wasn't sure what to think, other than that he didn't like it.

"I need to do this," Sam whispered, staring at the Keep. Evan faltered, following his gaze. He expected something there, something bad that had pulled Sam's attention.

But it was nothing, just the unfinished Keep. A testament to what could be, given enough time.

A place for defense of Chathem and the hope for his people.

Sam's reaction had ignited his curiosity. "What is it you hope to do?"

Sam blinked, then shook his head as if waking up from a dream. "Spring is coming soon. I can smell it in the air. We need to hurry before they come back. Will you give me what I need?" He turned back to Evan, imploring him.

So much of this man was a mystery to him, so much needed to be told. He wasn't comfortable not knowing, and remembered the advice of his former tutors and teachers about trusting those who would betray him.

But Sam hadn't betrayed him, not yet at least. He could have done it, taken him out at every opportunity. Evan shivered, remembering being surrounded on the wall.

Sam had protected him. He owed him his life, and a debt of gratitude that went far beyond it.

Still, he was hesitant to give him complete control, and was still stinging from the lack of an answer to his own question. "I will think about it."

13

A Fresh Supply

Sam bid the Duke goodbye but stayed on the wall thinking about what he said and the plans for the future.

He looked back at the unfinished Keep. She was a shell of what she had been, scavenged bones that were picked over like a vulture's meal.

It was a shame, and made him close his eyes, but when he did, he could see it complete, shining in the sun with the banner of Hornblood flying and flapping in the summer sun.

When he opened his eyes again it was gone, a leaf in the breeze.

What would it take to make it a reality? Something stirred inside him, but it wasn't the violent, angry thing that resided deep down inside.

It was something different. Almost...excited.

He glanced back over his shoulder, watching the logs dragged one by one along the road and into the castle, swallowed up through the gate.

A pang of regret for everything that they had lost in the attack, and one final look out to the north, then Sam left the walls into the castle courtyard.

As agreed upon, they were taking them next to the makeshift carpenter's workshop and cutting off the branches with axe and hatchet. Since the trees were bare from autumn they had no mess of leaves to move out of the way, but there were twigs and shards of wood everywhere.

Keiren was directing the flow of wood, rejecting the worst of the logs for the fires and keeping the best for the timber pile. The rest he was putting in a separate pile.

The men were looking healthier, no longer emaciated after a good night of feasting and a few days of eating well.

Sam hadn't expected Captain Silverthorn to leave at all, let alone so early. He didn't know what to think of that, other than that he wasn't sure who else would be able to train them other than himself.

"What do you have?" Sam asked.

"These would make good timbers, except there are a few questionable places that might not work well that I wanted you to take a look at. Ned or Archie would have known." A flash of sadness, or anger, went across Kerien's face.

Sam made a mental note to check the ones Kerien had cleared earlier, not wanting to do it in front of him. The man had been through enough that he wasn't sure how he would react to Sam going back over his work.

He was just glad that Kerien had expressed some doubt up front, glad that he hadn't overestimated his abilities.

"Good, if you can start dressing them into beams I'll take a look at this. Trent." Trent stopped chopping off branches and came to his side. "Help me with this."

Sam was glad for the work, something to keep his mind off the sinking feeling he was having that he would be back in charge of the training in less than a day or two.

The training sessions, after they had recovered enough to do so, had been short but intense. Captain Silverthorn was no stranger to training new recruits, that Sam could tell right away, but they had advanced beyond that designation a while ago.

Now, in addition to being masons and carpenters, they were proficient fighters able to handle the end of a sword and spear.

He thought about it in between logs. Most were good and sound, straight enough to be massaged into a beam or a column brace once the sapwood was trimmed back.

A few, however, had checks that were too big to overcome, or knots that ran too deep, and had to be cut up or sent to the firewood pile.

It was less than he was expecting though. Kerien had done a good job, considering the speed at which the logs were flowing. Every so often he would hear a distant crack, another tree falling in the forest.

It had taken them months to find the logs that had been lost in the fire, and most had been drying for a year. They didn't have that luxury now, and Sam didn't like it.

But did it really matter? The castle walls were built and firm. The gate was well constructed and just needed a bit of patching, and the Keep was finished enough to keep out any invaders who made it past those defenses.

"What will we use these for?" Trent asked as the timber piled up higher and higher. They had a few that were strong and long, promising for large beams or columns.

The question echoed his own in his mind. "I was planning on using them for the Keep."

"The Keep? We can't put them in this wet, can we?"

"The winter has dried them some, and they will yield most of their water within the next few months." Sam looked back up at the Keep, thinking of all they had pulled out and was lost.

Good, dry wood that had taken months to dress and install.

"Master Freeman, I don't understand." Trent's eyebrows were knitted in a furrow. "When will we use them?"

"Not until they are ready." Sam paused, wiping the bark from his hands. The movement of wood had made him warm, and he almost stripped off his outer coat. Sweat trickled down his back, tickling him all the way.

"But that will be years."

"For some, yes. But we must plan for the future."

"What future?" Sam's eyes snapped to Trent's. They were ablaze.

"The only future we have."

"If we stay here the only future we'll have will be death and blood." The vehemence in his tone surprised Sam.

"No."

"I've seen it, and I know it to be true." His own emotions roiled inside. It would be so easy to leave now, to slip out into the night and be gone.

It had been on his mind ever since the Hornblood soldiers had arrived.

"That may be true," Sam said, keeping his voice low. Trent had attracted the attention of the others and they were staring at them. "Do you want to be here, Trent?"

"I-I don't know."

"An honest answer. Here." Sam tapped a log. "Take this with me to the workshop. I've got a plan for it."

Trent nodded, then took his position on the other end. They pulled it into the workshop, wrestling it across two workbenches to prop it up.

But most importantly, to get out of earshot and prying eyes.

"I share your concern, and with what we have I wouldn't be sure we could stave off another siege." Sam sat on his stool, easing the pressure off his aching feet. His body wasn't used to the work and was still trying to recover. He took a swig from his water skin, refreshing water pouring down his throat.

"I've lived my life afraid of the Belmarch," Trent said. "But now that I've faced them in battle…"

"You aren't a soldier Trent, you're something else. I see it in you as I see it in myself."

Trent drew a deep breath, agony flashing across his face. "I didn't like killing them. It was…"

"No one should get used to it. I wish we hadn't been put in this position, but I've seen firsthand what these Belmarch can do, and I know why they chose this place to build this castle." Sam stood and picked up his hatchet, starting to cut the bark off the log.

"If we don't build this, what will happen to the rest of Chathem? Would they survive the onslaught of bloodthirsty men willing to do whatever it took?"

"No," Trent said, joining him. Their blades scraped against the wood. Fresh sap filled the air with its fragrance. "I have family to the south, my father and mother and sisters." He shook his head.

"There are things here that we love." Martha's face came to mind, then he shook it out of his vision. "There are men and women we have to protect here."

"I don't know if I can do it. I want to run."

"As do we all. You aren't the first to consider it, and you won't be the last, but this is our land and our home." A fire burned in his stomach, filling his body with its warmth. It counteracted the chill in the workshop. "I have a plan, and I think it will give us the best chance for survival."

"I'm sorry, I wish I wasn't so weak." Trent was holding back tears.

"You aren't weak," Sam said. "I've seen you up on the wall, standing your ground when other men would have fled. I've seen you build when it was too hot and cold, gone on when others would have quit. I see the strength that was in your heart and in your soul." He put down his hatchet and squeezed Trent's shoulder.

"I've seen weak men abandon their brothers on the battlefield, or leave before it even starts. No, you are not weak."

"You're one of the only reasons I haven't run away yet." Trent rubbed his eyes with a sleeve.

Sam was taken aback. "Me?"

"After all we've been through, you're still here and willing to do anything. I see it, the Duke sees it, and the Overseer saw it."

"You give me more credit than I am due."

"I've learned more than how to hold a plane and saw, or a sword."

Sam didn't like the way this was going, was uncomfortable with what seemed like high praise to him. He shifted, letting go of Trent's shoulder, and returned to his work.

The hatchet handle was warm, oiled after years of work by hands. Freshly sharpened, it cut through the bark like a hot knife through butter.

"I'm sorry if I said the wrong thing," Trent said, turning to the log as well.

"No, it isn't that." Sam shook his head, then held it with a hand. "I never set out to do this when I came here, to train someone I mean." He reflected for a moment. "But the more I think about it the more I realize how much of a blessing it has been."

The bark was scratchy and rough beneath his hand. The last few months had been so hard, and now this. He didn't know how to react or what to think, so he didn't.

Together, in silence, they finished de-barking the log, then returned out into the courtyard with the others in the fading light of the day.

Raltone savored the fresh spring air, delighted at the change in weather. Gone were the cold days of winter, and all the snow and ice that came with it.

"And a good riddance too," he said.

"What was that, mi'Lord?" Sable asked.

"Nothing, are they ready to move?" He cast a sneer in his young compatriot's direction, lest he think him weak.

"Ready for your order," General Granb said. He had been subdued and put in his place. Raltone smiled, this one he actually felt as the once favored General squirmed.

"And you, Sable?"

"Ready for your order." He didn't glance at Granb.

Good. They have grown even more distrustful of each other.

With the sun shining, and the snow melting, Raltone gave a quick nod. "Then set them on their way."

He sat back in his chair, relaxing on the balcony as orders were given and relayed. Far back behind the troops in front, the horns sounded.

Men in rows of three stepped into formation, tight lines that would flash as they marched by. Granb did have his ambitions, but the man knew who to pick to keep the men disciplined.

They marched by, a thousand feet stamping in unison. The sound was music to Raltone's ears, and he plucked a bit of meat from the plate to chew on.

It was tender, cooked just the way he liked it, and juice almost flowed out as he took a bite. Paired with his dark red southern wine, it was a delicious meal and it got him in the mood to make a few decisions.

"Bring me my consort, and make sure she looks good." He stood, raising his glass. Others on the balcony scrambled to join him, Granb and Sable included. "Today marks the day we finally rise up above our squabbles and infighting to take what is rightfully ours.

"We scrape and dig in the hard dirt and rock, barely eking out a living here only to have it taken by the early snows and harsh storms of winter. But now, we will take Chathem and their soft lands and soft people and make them our own as it is by right."

"By right," echoed the others, the anger he felt at it being taken away from them in their voices.

"So, drink up, and drink hearty, for we march not to battle, but to a war that they have been owed for generations. To the Belmarch!"

Troops tramped by, a seemingly unending supply of them, and Raltone drank deep, imagining the glory to come.

14

DESTINY

"Why did you bother me with this?" Evan rubbed his forehead, trying to massage away the headache that had developed there.

"Your Highness, how are we to do our best work with the ground so cold? It freezes the men's hands and makes it impossible to quarry."

"What happened to the stone that we had piled up in the courtyard? I seem to remember large stacks of them lining up along the eastern wall, and the western wall."

Bill smiled a greasy smile, but it didn't fool Evan. He had spent enough time in taverns and inns to know when men were trying to shirk their duty or weasel out of a gambling debt. He never thought that would come in handy when he was having his...fun on his nightly escapades.

"Not much of it is worth anything. Too cracked for foundation stone and too jagged for anything other than infill."

"I see." Evan sat back, glancing at the bar in the corner of the room. It might have been emptied long ago, but it never seemed to escape his notice.

Particularity in times like these.

"How long is it taking you to dress the stone then, if it's too rough to use in the walls?" *Had Rhys had to deal with this many excuses? Or is it just me?*

Bill's eyes widened, just a touch before he recovered. "Too long, Your Highness. And with the state the men are in, it's worse than quarrying new stone."

"Then you've solved your dilemma." Evan took up his pen and dipped it in the inkwell. "Quarry the stone, as cold as it may be, and continue the supply for the new defenses as directed." He wrote it down before Bill could recover and make more excuses. "I'll expect everything to be on schedule and as promised." Evan looked up, arching an eyebrow. "Unless what you promised wasn't right to begin with. That would be...unfortunate, as I see you're a man well respected among your peers. It would be a shame to demote you after such long service to my family."

Bill's eyes wandered up above him, exactly where Evan had hoped. It made him hate himself a little, relying on his family's weight, but what else could he do? He didn't have many choices out here.

"You're right, as usual, Your Highness." Bill bowed, scraping back and out of the room as quickly as he could while making his niceties.

When the door shut behind him, Evan sighed and slumped back. The ink had stained his finger, and even though he tried to wipe it off, it was still there, stinking of it too.

He rubbed his eyes, trying to clear his head. No wonder Rhys had wanted to get out of here, and no wonder he was so far behind. He hadn't believed the poor man before, that he was under-manned and low on resources, but now that they had to do this himself, it was exhausting.

And nerve-wracking.

Spring was just around the corner, and warmer weather would clear the passes in Belmarch and leave them vulnerable to attack. Like last time, he wasn't sure they would get any help from anyone down south.

He picked up his book on castle construction, thumbing through the masonry chapter again, trying to see where it had said anything about rough stone being useful for anything other than infill.

He had to read through the whole chapter to reassure himself that it wasn't true, that it didn't say that anywhere.

The question was if Bill said it because he was incompetent, or if he was lying to cover something else up.

It was hard to decide, but he couldn't well throw him over the wall. He was honest when he said he was held in good regard among the men, almost too good. He had cultivated his loyalty well, and the masons were thick in it.

It would have to be a hard fall from grace to drop his standing, and Evan thought of different ways of doing it.

Each time, he came up short.

Barger knocked at the door, a quiet rapping that was perfectly spaced. Evan bid him enter, then stood to stretch.

"Is it dinner already?" Evan asked, after greeting the man and receiving one in return.

"Yes, Your Highness." Barger set the meal on the table, a stew based on the smell coming from it, then went to tend to the fire.

"I wonder, what do you think of Bill?" Evan walked up to the table, but didn't sit at it. He kept a close eye on Barger out of the corner of his eye.

"The mason?"

"Who else?"

Barger poked at the logs glowing in the fireplace, shifting them around to make room for more. They hissed and spat at him. "What would you like to know about him?"

"How did he manage to earn his position?" Evan pushed away the irritation at not getting a good answer from him, and took off the cover. He was right, stewed vegetables and what might have been meat, but with a nice, fat, crusty roll alongside. "Seems young for a master mason."

"No one else wanted the position, from what I have heard." Evan took a bite as he listened, the roll crunching. Inside was soft and fluffy.

"No one?"

"No one who valued their life." With a careful touch he added a log, making sure it flared up before he stood. "Bill is a violent man, quite difficult to see unless you catch him at the right time. He tends to have others do his dirty work for him now."

"I see." Evan made a mental note to watch him more carefully. Barger stood, clasping his hands behind his back, then cleared his throat. "Go on then, as distasteful as I find it."

Barger slipped out a piece of paper and started going through the inventory. It wasn't as bad as Rhys had been, that man could have put a bear to sleep, but he still wasn't used to it.

Evan finished his meal and sat back, listening to the long list of supplies that had been brought in and added to the little they had.

By all accounts they were in a good position, plenty of arms and food, and well supplied for a garrison. The only problem was that they weren't a garrison.

"Thank you, and thank the cooks for me." Evan stood, pacing around his room, as Barger wrapped up his tallies and put them back in his pocket.

"Do you require anything else, Your Highness?" Barger had cleared the meal while he was pacing.

"No, nothing." Barger turned to leave. "Wait, there is something." Evan had been turning it over in his mind for quite some time now, a thorny problem he couldn't seem to put a finger on. "Why is it that Sam Freeman is in the position he's in?"

"Similar circumstances to Bill, I'm afraid. The previous master carpenter died in the same sickness that took the head mason."

"But he doesn't seem that...old."

"He isn't, from the rumors I've been told. Late thirties or early forties. What is the reason you have for this question, if you don't mind my asking, Your Highness?"

"I'm troubled. I don't know where he came from, or where his loyalties lie. He's a proficient fighter and a good leader but refuses to tell me or anyone else why that is."

"Perhaps it is because he does not want anyone else to know."

"And that's what troubles me." Evan stopped, turning short and pivoting on his heel. A log shifted in the fire, spitting and cracking. "Men who hide secrets are not to be trusted."

"Quite so, Your Highness." Barger was standing, heels together, watching attentively.

"I don't know why I brought you into this mess. You really shouldn't have anything to say on the matter." Evan sighed. "To be honest, I'm at a loss for advisers ever since Overseer Rhys left."

"Your time with Captain Silverthorn was not...productive?"

"Too much so." Evan walked to his seat, then slipped into it, leaning on his desk. "He gave me a long list of things to watch out for, things to do." He held up a note scribbled with markings and writing.

"It is the duty and honor of the Duke, I'm afraid." Evan knew that Barger was only humoring him, listening was his own duty. What he said or did afterward, Evan wasn't sure.

"Dismissed." Barger turned to go. "And Barger, thank you." He gave a deep bow, considering his package of dishes, and left Evan alone.

He sat, watching the fire for a while. Seeing the red and yellow battle with each other, tossing and lancing at one another in their quest to consume. The thick smell of pine smoke was in the air and curled up around the chimney, not all of it escaping up and out of the room, but Evan didn't mind. It had been too long without for him to not like it.

But his eyes kept wandering down to the note, a list that he appreciated and detested all in the same breath. He sighed, hoping the weight would roll off his shoulders and onto someone else.

That isn't my destiny. He rolled the word around in his mind, wondering what it really meant. *Destiny.*

Something he hadn't spent a lot of time considering, something barely spoken of in his childhood. A path that was chosen for him.

A good word for what I live. All the things he had given up, been forced to give up. A childhood alone, a youth spent the same way. Always wanting to be accepted, to have a friend, and always being told you were above them and must lead them one day.

It was no wonder I was driven to the drink. The hatred inside his breast grew and worsened then, a life of ease not so because of what he was called to do.

He wished he was back in the slums again, accepted by the very bottom members of society, or among the houses of ill repute. The women there didn't care who or what he was, only the color of his coin. He could buy friends for gold, and they would make his night shine.

That's what he'd told himself, but deep down he knew it was a lie. Those men and women were just as empty as he was, on as much of a search and journey as he.

Evan buried his hands in his head, staring at the words on the page.

"Train constantly for attack. Make sure the men know how to use the bows in the dark. Keep all openings shut and locked unless directly used for access."

All simple things, all things that had been drilled into him as a child that he had long put aside. Silverthorn, or his father, was always trying to remind him of his past.

Something he always wanted to forget.

Evan's throat was so dry every time he swallowed it was like sand scratching his throat. It wouldn't be much to summon Barger, to tell him to bring the wine. There was still a little bit left in the casks he had brought, and more that were sent with the arms. Not good stuff, from what he could gather, but enough to drown these problems for a night.

Just one night. Just one sip. After that it would be easy to stop. He had already done it for weeks now.

It was tormenting him, calling to him. Evan stood up, his hands shaking trying to hold it back.

He was going to fail. He was going to do it. Then, his eyes chanced to look upon his sword.

It too had been a gift from his father, along with the duty that was bound like a millstone around his neck.

Well balanced, sharp, a delight to hold, he was by it in an instant, holding onto it like a drowning man clutches at the tree branch floating by.

It was cold in his hands, soaking the warmth from his fingers, but it felt good. So good.

He drew it, the rasp from the scabbard ringing in his ears and filling the place the drink wanted to go.

He turned back into himself, losing himself in the forms. It had been too long, and he stumbled at points in the harder forms. So, he continued, starting over.

It wasn't much, but the pain of the workout reminded him of what was real, of why he couldn't regress. He couldn't drown his sorrows in wine, but he could drown them in his own sweat.

Soon, it came pouring out of him as he moved faster and faster, thrust after parry, swing after charge.

When he finished the last form, he stood gasping. His heart pounded, and he could only lean on his sword and stare up at the crest of the Hornbloods hanging above his desk.

"I will show him that this Hornblood still has life left in his veins. I will not give up."

15

THE MANTLE

As soon as Evan said the words he realized that had been in this place before. Alone, afraid, no knowledge of what to do.

But that time he had survived, managed to make it out of his room and into the world that surrounded him.

He took a deep breath, breathing in the smoke and the smell of ink and paper all rolled up into one. His hands brushed the leathery parchment, then grasped it.

It was a long list, and some of them he could never really be finished with.

"Always be vigilant?" It felt a bit silly talking to himself out loud, but he was alone in his room with no one to overhear.

Making up his mind, he tucked the paper into his pocket and sheathed his sword. He had caught his breath, and his heartbeat had slowed enough to be at a quick pace instead of pounding. It was time to make another visit.

Evan swept on his coat and strode out the door. Sounds of the cooks echoed down the corridor, through the open door at the end. They were talking, giggling, and laughing. It was a good, solid sound, and strengthened his resolve.

he passed by the kitchens, getting a glimpse in and sampling the wonderful aromas drifting out of it. There was meat, spiced heavily it smelled like, and cracking with fat. It made his mouth water and he swallowed it back.

No one gave him a second glance. *They are relying on someone to protect them.* His mother's face swam to his mind, and it brought a faint smile to his lips.

She was south of here, and to the west, deep in Hornblood territory and the Hornwood. She had slipped in a package for Silverthorn to deliver.

It was still in his room, a bundle that felt suspiciously like books. Another gift to strengthen him, or so she would have said.

The sun was sinking as he entered the courtyard, and the chill of the night was blowing in from the north. Evan kept one hand on the hilt of his sword but tightened his collar and turned to the carpenters' workshop.

He wasn't sure why he had to go there, other than that's where he thought Sam would be.

He was right, but the other two were there also. Evan wasn't sure of their names, but they stared at him as he opened the flap and strode inside. In the distance the masons' hammers rang and sang.

"Good evening, Your Highness," they said when they had recovered from their shock. Evan returned their greetings and turned to Sam, who still had a plane in his hand.

"I wish to speak with you." Evan glanced at the others. "In private."

Sam nodded, and the other two packed up their tools and left them. Evan waited until the sound of their boots was gone, taking a seat on a stool that was covered in wood shavings, after cleaning it off.

"To what do I owe the pleasure?" Sam smiled, more baring of teeth than a real smile. He tried to cover it quickly. "I apologize for the...tone. It's been a long day."

"It's been a long year," Evan said. "And what I'm about to ask for will make it longer, for you."

"Me only?"

"If you agree to it, I suspect it will affect a great many more." Evan leaned forward. "Why did you come here?"

Their eyes locked. Something passed over Sam's face, and through his eyes. Evan couldn't put a finger on what it was. It was emotions, but what emotions?

He wasn't going to let him get out of this question and stared without blinking.

"That's... a good question." Sam brushed at the section of wood before him. Shavings fell to the floor, added to the growing pile.

Evan was uncomfortable but had to know the answer. The silence stretched on as Sam dropped his gaze to the table before him, working out the answer to the question.

"In some ways I think it is a way to atone for what I've done." Sam shook his head. "But I'm not sure about that anymore either. I have this...this urge inside me that I can't seem to satisfy. I thought coming here would help."

Evan wasn't sure that was what Sam was going to say, and he scrutinized the man further, but no additional explanation was given.

"You signed up for this, you know what you owe."

"I do."

"Then I would ask that you function as the Overseer, in Rhys' absence."

Sam's eyes flashed back up. "Your Highness, I couldn't. I don't know how to build a castle."

"Neither, I suspect, did he," Evan said. "And neither can I. If you don't do it, take up this mantle that I've laid upon you, then who exactly will?"

That caused him anguish. "I know many good men that could, and all of them are in the ground."

What should he do? Evan saw the conflict in the man's eyes and in his heart. His father would have counseled a heavy hand, perhaps, to order him to it.

But he wasn't his father. He wasn't his mother. Evan had to accept that he had to be his own man.

"I've woken up in too many ditches to count, done things to fritter away my youth that would make a woman of the night blush," Evan said, capturing Sam's attention.

"Your Highness, why are you telling me this?" It only added to the man's visible anguish.

"I'm no better than you. I happened to be born to a certain man and woman and that gives me the right to rule. The duty," Evan spat, "to rule. But I don't know how to do that, and I've spent years trying to run from it. So, you can either help me learn, or you can watch as the Belmarch wash over us without stopping, burning and killing everything and everyone we ever loved."

Sam stared at him, eyes wide and jaw dropped.

"What do you have to say?"

"Your Highness, I -" Sam snapped his jaw shut, then turned away from him. "I don't know what to say."

"Say yes, and then we can be done with it."

"It isn't that easy."

"No, I'm afraid it isn't." The fire was dying down, but it still gave its heat and light to the room. Evan waited for Sam to continue, examining everything else while he did.

It was a place of work, that he was sure. There were no frills or art to speak of, it was a plain as a monk's room, but everything was solidly built. The workbenches were stout and had good, thick legs, and were filled with tools of all kinds.

"When I came to this place, I expected to be a simple laborer." Sam spoke, his back still to him. "A way to...get away from what I had become. And what I was going to be."

Evan leaned back, the stool creaking under his shifting weight. It wasn't the most comfortable, far more spartan than his own carved wooden chair with cushions, but it beat being on his feet. The light from the day was dying, not as early as it had been.

The bell rang then, calling everyone to evening formation.

"It is time to make a decision, Sam Freeman." Evan stood, tightened his coat about him again.

"It's all so much to think about." Sam turned back to him but didn't meet his eyes. He put away his tools, and the tools of the others, walking around the workshop and doing anything but consider his proposition. "I have to admit, I'm overwhelmed. Will you give me some time, to think about it?"

He needs time. Didn't I need time too? Evan suppressed the bit of vexation he felt. It was an honor, one that should rightfully go to nobility. *Can't he see what kind of risk I am taking?*

"A night. No more. Think about it and give me your answer tomorrow." Sam had finished with the tools, everything in a place that had some sense of order, even if Evan couldn't figure out what it was.

"You are too kind, Your Highness. I will think on it, and I will think well." Sam clutched his hands.

Evan waited for him to go, to leave the workshop and enter the courtyard. "Aren't you to help lead the exercises?" he asked, when it was clear that Sam was staying.

"Yes, yes of course." Sam pulled his coat from a hook near the entrance flap, fumbled with the button at the top, and then finally managed to get it fixed. "They will be back, won't they?"

Evan chewed on his bottom lip, then stopped as soon as he realized he was doing it. "Every day I wonder if they will be on the horizon. When they come back, it will be with an army."

Sam let out a deep breath. "I was afraid I was the only one who thought so." He gave a simple bow, but one well practiced. *A clue to his past, perhaps?*

"Goodnight, Duke Hornblood." And when Evan had returned the greeting, he was gone.

Evan followed, breathless into the evening twilight. The sunset had faded and the gloom of the night was nearly complete, but there was still the haze of glow spread out over the castle walls that made everything hard to see.

He crunched through the thinning snow, listening to the sounds of men assembling and talking in the yard. The clink of practice swords, a laugh here and there, and the squad leaders yelling at them to get into their positions all echoed around the courtyard, bounced from wall to wall.

The smell of sweat would soon be filling the air, mingling with the woodsmoke and hint of spring on the fading evening breeze. Evan stopped in the shadow of the Keep to watch them, keeping well out of sight in order to observe and think by himself.

Silverthorn had given a few pointers to the guards that made up the squad leaders, and they soon had all the workers assembled in nearly straight rows and columns. From there pairs were divided and set against one another.

They practiced sparring forms as Evan watched. His mind wandered to the south, to the fertile lands that they protected that had long ago been stripped of forest and tree.

Were they too soft from years of peace? Did they not see the enemy that was on their doorstep?

But Evan had to be honest with himself, neither did the Hornbloods. His father had sued for the right to build the castle, but from what he remembered it was only a precaution. He thought the internal power struggles and infighting would keep them at bay for years.

And so, Evan had believed so too. Maybe that's why his father had sent him here to be in charge, to be safely out of the way while the King called for his forces to be sent east and south to fight those raiders.

He turned the thought over in his mind, unsure of what it meant or why it mattered. His conversations with Silverthorn returned to him, time spent listening to words from a trusted adviser to his father that seemed to mean little to him.

Particularly his parting words.

He tried to dismiss them, to focus on observing the men. At first, he was successful. The steam was rising off them, and they were shedding outer garments as they trained. They had shifted from sparring practice to full-fledged fighting, striking and kicking and punching in order to bring the other man down to his knees.

And they weren't holding back either. It looked like some were locked in mortal combat, but as soon as a squad leader came over to finish the fight they released each other.

Evan was surprised at how much better they were than when he first came. Those first nights, where he had watched Yand train them surreptitiously from the shadows, were an abomination.

Now, however, they looked as though they might have a chance to stand their ground, given the right protection and advantage. They were still far from professional fighters, but they wouldn't be useless in battle.

Battle. *Is that what is coming?*

There was something on the night air, now still. A force of some kind was growing in the north, he could feel it. A storm was brewing, and it meant to come south and sweep them from their position and into Chathem.

And the only thing standing in between Belmarch and Chathem was this castle.

Evan looked to the north, shivering in the night air, and was afraid.

16

A Meeting in the Kitchens

Sam attacked Trent, pressing his advantage in arm reach with powerful strokes. Each one knocked Trent's sword away, but somehow he managed to bring it back into blocking position before the next one landed.

There was fear on his face, a real fear, which made Sam realize what he was doing. His muscles were starting to regain their former strength, and he stopped as the end of the round was called.

Sweat trickled down the side of his nose and he wiped it away as he made his bow. Trent's eyes were wide.

"Did I do something wrong?" he asked in a whisper.

Blood was pounding through his ears, fed by the thing that waited inside and the anger that was brought up by the Duke. "No," he said curtly. "I'm sorry, I should have held back more, but you did well."

That thing wanted to crunch and snap, and was almost awake, but Sam had managed to control it somehow.

Mathew was up now, calling an end to the night's training. His blood still roared in his ears, even though he had managed to get some control of his breathing, and Sam didn't feel like sticking around to talk with any of the others, as they were apt to do following the training sessions.

"Keep working on the forms," Sam said, clasping Trent's arm and trying to smooth out his rough treatment. "You've done well to improve, but there is always someone stronger and faster that will end your life if you let them."

"I will."

Sam nodded, then caught what he had said. He gave a curt good night then turned and walked back to the Keep. His mind was ablaze.

Overseer of the castle? I couldn't do that. He knew someone else should have the position, would do a better job, but when he tried to think of who he came up short.

Bill was too power hungry. Mathew too green. None of the carpenters were even remotely ready. Dale wouldn't care.

He had to talk to someone about this, and Dale first came to mind, but when he went to the forge it was empty and cold, so he trudged back to the Keep.

The only other person he wanted to talk to about it, who was still alive, he thought might be in the kitchen.

But he was too strung up and angry to go see her first, so he paced the halls and stairs, going up and down and around where he knew he could find her.

As his heart rate slowed and his breathing normalized, Sam soon found that he wasn't walking to calm down any more, but out of nervousness.

What will she think? What will I say? Sam clasped his fingers and put them behind his head, trying to rationalize the state he was in.

"Don't be a coward," he said to himself, "Just go see her." Squaring up, he marched through the empty great hall and down the corridor to the kitchen.

And then stopped just outside the door.

He couldn't do it. It felt like there was a chasm between him and the door. He tried to raise his hand and open it, but it wouldn't respond.

Sam was just about to turn around and flee when it banged open, making him jump.

"What are you doing out here, sneaking around?" Martha was waving a spoon in his face, but then stopped as soon as she saw who it was. "Sam! I thought you were a little one trying to sneak a midnight snack."

"Sorry to disturb you." Sam swallowed, then stuffed his hands in his pockets. *It's done now, no use trying to run away.* "May I... join you?"

"Come in," she said with a smile, and he followed her in, checking the corners. They were alone and she pulled out a little stool for him to sit in by the fire, getting another for herself and bidding him sit.

His senses were assaulted by the thousand and myriad of smells and tastes that lived in the kitchen. Breads, meat, vegetables among all the herbs and spices that were shipped in with the resupply. It helped distract him as Martha offered to make him something warm to drink.

"Now then, what brings you to see me?" Her eyes twinkled in the low burning light of the fire, banked down for the night. Sam felt warm inside and was warmed by its heat.

"I had to talk to someone, and I was hoping to catch you."

"Whatever is the matter?" Her smile slipped as she watched him. "You look-"

"Martha, I've been asked to do something that I don't think I can." His face felt tight, and he tried to relax it. His entire body felt strung up, like a string stretched tight. "I don't know what to do."

"What have you been asked to do?" Her voice was quiet and soothing, and she leaned forward.

What am I thinking? I can't tell her. He was in agony, and she looked so beautiful in the soft light that it made it worse.

She's no longer a wife. The flash of a thought made him squeeze his eyes shut, then put a hand over them. He took a deep breath.

"The Duke asked me to be the Overseer." It was out, there was no taking it back now.

He wanted desperately to look at her, but he couldn't bring himself to.

"How do you feel about that?" He glanced up, met her eyes. She didn't seem surprised, or even disgusted like he thought she would. There was no disapproval in those eyes, only reassurance.

"I couldn't do it."

"Why not?" she asked, voice soft and low. So different from the commanding voice she yielded like her spoon with the other women.

He thought she would have been judgmental, that she would have agreed with him and urged him to say no, even though he didn't see a way how. This, though...

This was not what I expected. He didn't have an answer for her and struggled to find one. She waited patiently. "I don't know how."

"So, learn."

"It isn't that easy."

Martha shrugged, then captured a stray bit of hair that had come loose, brushing it behind her ear. "I didn't say it would be easy."

"But don't you see how impossible it is?" Sam stood up and turned away, stroking his chin. "I can't be in charge of the castle, that should be someone else."

"Should it be me?" He spun at her question, a hint of undercurrent in her tone. He dare not think of what it was.

But she was smiling a half smile, hiding it well. "Or should it be... Bill?" she asked.

"You know that would be a disaster, and its exactly what he wants. I think that's the reason he chose the Overseer to leave."

Her eyes widened in real surprise. "He chose the Overseer?"

Sam stepped back, bringing up his hands, and stammered "I didn't mean to say that. Promise me you won't tell anyone else about it."

Her eyes were narrow now, and she was almost out of her seat. White-knuckled hands clenched around her spoon. "What have you been up to?"

"It was the Overseer's choice, but Bill wanted him gone too. He wouldn't help me with the boat unless I agreed to it."

"That dirty, rotten scoundrel." Her smile was twisted into a scowl now. "Always scheming and scraping about. What else did you agree to?"

He had shrunk back, but now that he had gathered his wits Sam straightened. Martha was half his size. *I shouldn't be this afraid of her.*

"That's not what I came to talk about. I'll tell you later, another time, when I don't have the weight of the castle on my shoulders."

Her scowl faded at the reminder but didn't disappear. "You take my advice Sam Freeman, you be careful around that snake." She sniffed. "And as for you feeling like you can't do this or that I want you to stop it and start acting like a man."

Martha rose and advanced. It took all he had to stand firm. "If you can think of someone else who can do it tonight, then you tell him no. If, however, you come up short like you have for however long you've been thinking on it then you know the answer you have to give."

She was next to him now, near enough he could smell the sweat and cooking on her, and the unique smell that only she had. "But I don't know how to do it."

"And you'll learn, just like everyone else learns when they don't know how. I didn't know how to bake and cook or lead a kitchen, and now see how the girls are in their place."

"Martha, half those women are your age or older."

"Which makes it worse. They should know what to do and how to do it without my direction, but still, they need it." Her face softened. "Just like all those men out there need someone to lead them."

"I'm no leader either."

"Which makes you the best man to do the job." She was so close, he could almost feel the heat coming off of her. Her eyes were so soft in the light, her lips looked so supple. Martha reached up and smoothed a wrinkle in his shirt. "Sam," her voice was almost a whisper now. "I have to tell you something."

His heart was pounding. She hadn't taken her hand off his chest. Her touch was so soft, and he wanted to reach up and take her hand, lift her chin.

He cracked open his suddenly dry mouth. "What is it?"

"I-" She blinked, peering up at him from underneath her lashes.

He was drawn down to her, felt lightheaded and anxious. The lock of hair fell back over her eyes.

Sam reached out and brushed it back behind her ear.

The door slammed open, two girls bursting in laughing and giggling. Martha's head whipped around, and she snatched her hand away.

Sam pulled back too, heart pounding and breathing heavily. The two girls went silent, the air filled with an oppressive awkwardness.

"We're sorry mistress Martha," one of the girls murmured. They were clasping arms and looking down at the floor.

Martha looked as if she had seen a ghost and busied herself with putting her hair up. "What are you two doing down here at this hour?"

"We came to put away the vegetables for tomorrow," the younger one said, holding up a basket filled with dried potatoes and turnips. "We didn't mean to..."

"I'll have none of that," Martha marched up to them. Sam wanted to crawl into a hole and die somewhere, anywhere but here.

The door was still open and called to him as a possible means of escape, but all three of the women were in between it and him.

"Sam and I were just talking about something that need not concern you," she continued, rummaging around in the basket, then finally snatching it from them. "Now, go on and get gone. Off with you." She shooed them away, and they made a short curtsy and turned to go, but they kept sending darting glances his way.

Sam wasn't sure what to do, his hands itched, and his feet didn't seem to want to move. "Yes, Martha and I weren't doing anything," he said, then started to blush at how bad it sounded as it came out of his mouth. She turned slowly and stared at him, eyes almost bulging.

The girls were fighting to keep smiles off their faces as they turned and left in silence. The tension didn't leave with them though, it lingered.

"I'm sorry I bothered you so lately," he stammered, making for the door.

"You don't need to go," Martha said, reaching out for him. Sam couldn't stand being inside the kitchen for another minute though and made a beeline for the door. "Wait, Sam!"

He stopped in the doorway, grasping the rough wooden frame for dear life, holding onto it to keep him afloat. "I'm sorry, I shouldn't have caught you up in this. It was my burden to share, not to give to anyone else, and it will be my burden to bear."

"You put too much of it on your shoulders," she said, voice cracking. "You don't have to try and bear it alone."

He wanted to turn, to catch her up in his arms and hold her, wipe away the tears that he knew were streaming down her face.

But, he couldn't. "Goodnight, Martha," he said, then left.

17

CHILDISH DREAMS

Evan watched the men finish their training for the night and slipped into the Keep before they returned. Back in his room, he went through his new evening ritual.

First, he took out his sword and practiced each of the forms Yand had spent so many years teaching him. By now he was smooth with each one, and was tempted to go through the motions, but something in Yand's training kept him from doing that.

It must have been Yand himself, and how he always seemed so intense when he was training, completely focused on one movement after the other.

His muscles felt better afterward, the kinks worked out of them, but he was tired. He selected a book, the Histories again, and sat in his chair next to the fire to read.

It was his fourth time reading it, at least, and he finished a few chapters before putting it away.

He fingered the spines of each book on his bookshelf, but glanced at the package from his mother he still had yet to open.

She had known him so well, he wondered what she had given him. *Why have I waited so long to open it?*

He suspected there was news from home, and that was what kept him away. What could possibly be so bad that his mother would send to him?

Or perhaps it was a letter from his father, finally disowning him after one too many failures. Evan shivered despite the pleasant temperature of the room. There was a pit in his stomach, a feeling of dread.

But it might be good news for all I know. Curiosity grew, bigger than his fear, and finally he could take it no longer.

Evan crossed the room and picked it up, the smooth oilskin wrapping left residue on his fingers. With one pull he tugged open the string and let it fall, revealing the contents inside.

There was a letter at the top, folded neatly into four and a perfect square, his mother's handwriting spelling out his full name.

She rarely used his full name, but in official correspondence she was a stickler for protocol. The dread grew.

He pushed it off to the side and picked up the plush red leather-bound book, and its mate underneath.

There was no title emblazoned on the front, or the side, but when he opened it, there was a beautiful scribe's handwriting. *Tales of the Eventide.*

The second was its companion, a second volume. Evan had never heard of them, and was completely befuddled. *Why these?*

With a glance back at the letter, which he let lie, he took his two new books back to the fireplace.

Starting at the beginning, and placing the second volume off to the side, Evan took up the deeply leather smelling book and started reading.

Pages turned with a simple rustle, complemented by the gentle murmur of the fire as it pulled air up the chimney with it. Evan fell into those tales, and didn't come out until the very last page.

When he did, he blinked. The fire had burned low, almost out, and Barger was standing at his side.

"Is everything all right, Your Highness?"

"Yes," Evan said, shutting the book softly. His eyes wandered over to the second volume, wondering if they told of the same great heroes from old. "Confused, that's all."

"It is late, I was wondering when you would retire."

"Is it now?" Evan glanced at the letter on his desk. "I think I'll go to bed then and save this one for tomorrow."

Barger nodded, then banked the fire down for the night. Evan watched him, in a daze, and as he was about to go grabbed his arm.

"Do you believe them?"

"Believe what, Your Highness?"

"Any of the old stories?"

Barger shook his head and smiled wanly. "I was never fond of them, and no one really told me any."

"Surely that couldn't be true," Evan said, letting go of the poor man. "Even my mother told me stories when I was younger, of knights in shining armor coming in to kill the beast guarding the princess and win her heart."

Barger stood stiffly. "Not all men are given the opportunity, Your Highness." His voice was calm, but empty of emotion like he had squeezed a sponge out.

"I want to think they are true, that they could be," Evan said. "But I gave up hope that I would be that knight long ago."

"Childish dreams die when you grow older," Barger said. Evan felt the exhaustion flood over him then and noticed it in Barger's face too. The man was worn out, and not just from the winter.

"I don't understand why my mother sent these to me." Evan picked up the books and presented them. He waved over to the bookshelf. "She sent so many practical books, things that I suspect she thought I would need, but these are meant to be told to children."

"I would not know the mind of the Duchess, Your Highness."

"I think you do, and I think you would. So many times you know my mind better than I know myself that it scares me. Always there with the right thing at the right time, ready without my asking."

"I have been in your service many years," Barger said, still cold and toneless.

"And you have seen me with my mother those same years."

"Your Highness, I should leave." Barger made a motion to go to the door, but Evan stopped him, rising from his chair.

"Now then, you're here now and I need you. Why would my mother send these?"

Barger held up his hands in defeat. "I couldn't say."

"Make a guess."

"The Duchess may have told you why she did it."

Evan cocked his head to the side. "What makes you think that?"

"The letter, Your Highness." Barger motioned to the desk, pointed it out. Evan narrowed his eyes, and examined Barger closer. That letter had only been there this night.

"If you like, I can stay here while you open it." Barger relaxed into a more natural position as Evan considered it.

An owl hooted outside. "Yes," Evan said, knowing that it meant he would be forced to open it.

He wasn't sure why he was so reticent. It was his mother, not his father, or so he hoped.

Evan slowly went over to the desk as Barger patiently waited. He picked up the letter, turning it over in his hands. The Hornblood seal was pushed into the wax, a light touch of his mother's ring.

He brushed his thumb across it, smooth and waxy. The ridges were stark in feel against the rest of it.

Glancing up at Barger, who stared at him with a blank face, Evan took up his knife and cut it in a swift strike.

It was open now, and he unfolded it, relieved to see his mother's writing.

Evan sat back in the chair and read.

"What is it, Your Highness?"

He glanced back up at Barger, who wore a look of concern. "My father's been wounded."

It was so strange to think of him, so strong and able, now confined to a bed.

Evan felt lightheaded, and leaned back. His world was spinning. He had never even considered his father could be in such a position.

"I'm sorry to hear that."

"I-I'd like a drink."

"At once." Barger was gone in an instant, out the door, leaving him alone.

Evan clutched at the letter, re-reading it twice more. It was true, it had to be. That was her gentle handwriting, her graceful signature.

The door creaked open, a soft tinkling as Barger entered carrying a tray with a cup on it. Steam rose, obscuring the fire, from the lip.

"Here you are." He set the cup in front of him, but Evan was distracted, carried away in his thoughts. "Would you like me to take it away?"

"What?" He noticed the cup then. "No, thank you." Evan's shaking hand hit the side of it. *What if he dies? What would I do then?*

"She wants me to stay here." The cup was warm, almost too hot for his hands.

"Careful, Your Highness, that just came from the kettle." Barger was still staring at him, waiting on him.

Evan realized he was about to take a big mouthful of it and stopped. It smelled of willow bark. It must have been the tea that came with the soldiers.

He took a sip, scalding his tongue in the process, but the tea brought him to his senses. "Thank you." He blew on it to cool it down, taking another smaller sip that only flooded his mouth with warmth.

The feeling traveled down his throat to his stomach, which by now was turning upside down. "What if he dies? What would happen to me then?" Evan put the cup back down and rose, pacing around his room at a furious pace.

His exhaustion was gone now, he couldn't sleep. She had tried to make it gentle, soft even, but he could tell that he was hurt badly. Too badly.

"May I suggest that it might not be as bad as it seems?"

"You don't know her like I do." Evan shook his head, wiping back his hair. He wanted something stronger. He needed a drink. His throat felt like sandpaper.

But there was none in the room, and he knew that Barger wouldn't go get some.

I could go myself. "I'm not ready to be the Archduke. I can barely function now. I can't even keep the castle safe."

"Was there any other news?" Barger was following him, at a loss for how to help him. Evan didn't know what he needed himself, other than a cool glass of wine.

No, get hold of yourself.

"I need to go." Evan grabbed his sword and coat and headed for the door. "Don't wait up for me."

He walked down the corridor and through the Keep, turning left intentionally to keep away from the stairs that led to the cellar.

They kept the alcohol down there, at his request, and he wasn't sure what he would do if he went down there, but he knew he wouldn't be able to resist it if he saw it.

He almost stopped at the kitchen, knowing there might be a stray barrel or two, but pushed by, going out the door into the bitter cold of the night.

Snow was falling, soft flakes that stuck in his hair and on his shoulders, and he took a moment to wrap his coat around his shoulders.

He wandered listlessly around the courtyard at first, then up to the walls. He touched it, feeling the cold soak up the warmth of his body, the roughness of the rock, and stared up at the top of it.

They aren't protecting me, they're trapping me inside. His entire life he had been trapped, no choice of friends, no choice of profession, not even a choice of who he would one day marry.

Everything was prescribed for him, a path that was laid out before he was ever born.

And now that path might be even closer than he realized. His entire family was counting on him now.

With a chill, he realized that his father might be dead even now, and a strange feeling of sadness accompanied it. He thought for a long time that he would be relieved when his father was gone.

Now, he was realizing what that would mean. It would mean an end to his simple life and the start of one much bigger. One filled with endless drivel and pressure too powerful to resist.

Evan pulled out his sword, turning back to the courtyard and the training grounds. He slipped into the first form, using it to clear his head.

Thrust. Parry. Strike. Thrust. Parry. Strike.

The sword was an extension of his body, another part to manipulate, just like Yand had taught him.

Thrust. His father was going to die. Strike. He would become the Archduke. Parry. He would be in charge of all of Hornblood.

The Ironwood. The Tree of Everling. Everything.

He broke out in a cold sweat, pushing away the thought even as he continued with his training.

The moon glinted off his blade as he spun. The forms melded into each other, and he sped up, trying to keep hold of his sanity.

He didn't know where he was going. He didn't know what to do.

And there was no one to guide him.

He kept going until his muscles ached and his lungs screamed, until his arms were shaking with the effort of holding up his sword, and then he pushed harder.

Legs shook, numbed by the cold, until he could finally hold it no longer. The sword clanged in the snow.

And Evan fell to the ground after it, eyes staring up at a cloudy night sky.

18

DEVOURING TREE

Snow fell around him, blanketing the courtyard in a silent, soft deafening. Evan blinked as a solitary snowflake fell in his eye and quickly melted.

His breath rose in big, white clouds that seemed black in the light of the moon, and he wondered what he was going to do.

When he caught his breath he got back up, out of the freezing snow, and went back to his room.

The Keep was quiet, almost everyone asleep by now, and he met not a soul on his way. He went to his room, stripped off his wet clothes next to the crackling fire that filled him with heat, and went to bed.

That night he had strange dreams, that he was at the Tree of Everlong leading the Midnight Watch, his mother and father standing with his grandparents that had long passed from this earth and watched.

He had no voice, but everyone seemed to be listening to him, and when he tried to turn around the great tree had turned into a monster, a gaping wide maw filled with rows of wooden fangs waiting as a tree branch arm grabbed him around the waist and pulled him inside to eat him.

Evan woke up in a sweat before the monster could kill him, heart pounding nearly out of his chest.

The fire had died down, leaving his room chilly, and he gathered the blankets back up around his body.

It was another day, another step closer to the duty he had spent his whole life running from. The sense of dread that his father might be dead hung on him, clung to him like a bad smell, and he found he could sit in his bed no longer.

Cold stone sucked the heat from his feet when he stood, and he jumped over to dress and get ready for the day.

There was no sign of Barger, and a quick glance told him it was still dark outside. It had been a short night.

And he felt it.

His body was still tired from the late night training session, but his eyes were bleary and heavy from the lack of sleep.

Evan went back to his study to re-read the letter, hoping everything from the night before was part of his nightmare, but it was still true.

The books seemed like some kind of sick joke now that he looked at them. He still had no clue why his mother had sent them.

To remind me of something? To teach me something? If so, what could a group of stories ever teach him?

He spent the time until breakfast reading his books on military tactics. When Barger entered the room, he wasn't sure how to treat him.

"Good morning, Your Highness." Barger was perfectly cordial and seemed to show no hint of the awkwardness that Evan himself felt.

He pursed his lips, unsure of whether he should bring it up or let the ruse go on. "Any word today?"

"The inventory is in progress, and we should have updated numbers this afternoon." Barger made his place at the table and stood by while Evan took his seat and started eating. "If you mean did anyone notice anything last night, I do not believe so."

He turned and tended the fire as Evan crunched on some toast, a small portion of butter covering it. It was crispy on the outside, but a bit burnt along the edges. Evan frowned at it, but then let it go.

Barger poked at the fire, getting great leaping flames working at the unburned portions of the logs, and soon had it crackling merrily. It warmed Evan from its heat, but it didn't banish the feeling of fear from his nightmare.

"We aren't ready." Evan stared into the flames, watching them shake and dance. "And we need to be."

"Your Highness?"

"Bring Sam Freeman to me. I want to speak to him." Barger nodded, then bowed.

Evan finished his meal while he waited, but he didn't have to wait long. A few minutes later the door opened and Barger admitted Sam, who greeted him and stood in front of his desk.

"You were supposed to give me an answer." Evan walked to his desk and sat, leaning back under the crest.

"I still feel that I am not the right man for the position," Sam said.

"My father is dead."

"The Archduke? I'm sorry..."

"Or might as well be, and we have the Belmarch breathing down my neck on their way to destroy everything. I don't have time for your self-doubt," Evan took a deep breath, calming himself. "We don't have time for your doubt now. Either take the position or leave."

Anguish played across Sam's eyes, but Evan thought he was going to say yes anyway. He finally nodded.

"Good. Now that we've got that out of the way we have some planning to do." Evan motioned to the chair, and Sam sat. "We have a lot of work to do, and I want to be ready. The Belmarch are going to remember who the Hornbloods are after they meet us."

The look of concern faded from Sam's face, and a hint of a smile played at his lips. "Very well, Your Highness. Where do we start?"

"You can get started on the work immediately." His chair creaked as the Duke leaned forward.

"Before we go further, Your Highness."

"What is it?" The Duke had reached out and was about to pull his book back.

"How long will you expect me to perform this job?"

The Duke paused and looked up. "I imagine if Rhys comes back, you would be released from it. Or, if a suitable replacement is found."

"That is my concern."

"Ah." The Duke put the book back, then reconsidered and shut it. "I can't say for sure what I think happened to Rhys, but in the event that he...hasn't survived, I give you my word that I will have a replacement sent. My father will know someone, or have one in mind, to take the position."

Sam exhaled, relieved that this would not continue in perpetuity. "I'm not sure where to start."

"Take Rhys' office, look through what he left. He gave me some instruction that I can pass on, but a bulk of his work is in the records there."

"His office? I couldn't do that."

"You'll have to. After lunch we'll go over what I know. You can meet me here." The Duke took up his book again, and Sam happened to catch a glimpse of the spine.

Boat building? He could have used that a long time ago. *What is the Duke of Hornblood doing with a book on boat building?*

"Is there anything else?" The Duke was peering at him from over the cover.

Sam swallowed. "No, Your Highness." he was dismissed, and started to leave.

"Wait, you'll need his key." The Duke rummaged through his pockets and produced a large, brass key. Sam went back and took it. It was cool, and smooth.

He left with it in hand, and stared at it out in the hallway. This was a place he never expected to be in, a situation beyond all imagination just a few months before.

But there was little he could do about it now, and Sam went there reluctantly. He stopped outside the big, brown door, remembering that he helped build it.

And now, his new task lay within. Fear and dread ran through him. He didn't know how to oversee anything, let alone a castle, but then he had not been a carpenter before either.

Nor had he always been a fighter.

He slipped the key into the lock and turned. There was resistance, and he pushed, then it was through as the lock clicked back.

He pushed the door opened and went inside. It was dark, and quiet. A layer of dust had accumulated on the ground and his feet left prints as he fumbled about.

Finally, he found the tinderbox where he remembered Rhys had kept it and lit a candle. There were no windows in this place, and it had a dank, musty smell. Water dripped down the chimney, from melting ice perhaps.

Sam examined the room. Rhys had left it fairly well cleaned up, with a stack of papers tied with string on one side of the desk. His possessions were still strewn about the room, but in their places in cupboards and shelves.

I won't be touching those. It felt eerie and oppressive. He kept glancing to the desk, and what would certainly be the records.

"Sam?" He turned. Martha was in the doorway, arms across her chest. She was peering in, squinting into the dim room.

"Martha." He didn't know what else to say.

"I thought you would be here, after what you said last night." She stepped one step into the room. "I hope..." Her face was drawn, and she looked older than she was.

"No," he said, looking around the room. "No, not at all. I mean, will you have a seat?" He found a chair and pulled it out for her.

"Yes. I'd like that. We've been so busy with lunch." He set it out for her, and she slipped into it. "I brought some wood. I wasn't sure if anyone had refilled it since he left."

Sam was touched. *Had she thought of him, or was it a habit, always making sure everything was in its place?* He tried to get a good look at her face, but it was hidden in the shadows.

She told him it was in the hall, and he brought it into the room and filled the fireplace. He cut a few starters off and coaxed a fire up, feeding it carefully and keeping it away from the drips until it was big enough to turn them to steam.

With some effort he soon had it burning, and added a few more logs until it burned strong and bright, casting an orange glow into the room and banishing some of the dank.

Water dripped down and sizzled, turning to steam to mix with the sweet smelling smoke that was sucked up the chimney and out of the room.

Martha was watching him, now lit up by a healthy glow. She had gained back some weight, and he was glad to see how much healthier she looked.

And there was something about her face as he watched it in the soft glow. It turned his stomach into knots and dried out his mouth.

"I should-" he stammered, wanting to continue, "about last night, I mean-"

He felt lightheaded and giddy. *I'm not a boy of fifteen anymore.* "What I mean to say is..."

"You aren't good with words?"

"No, that's not it." His head shot back to look at her. She had a hint of a smile. It melted the stern look she usually wore and made her seem about three years younger.

Then, as he stared, she furrowed her brows. "What is it? Is something wrong?"

"Yes. I mean no-" *Come on, Sam, you've been in dangerous places with less fear than this.* He took a deep breath, trying to calm the flutter in his heart. "What happened the other night. I didn't mean to take advantage of you like that. It wasn't right, and I wanted to apologize."

Her eyes opened wider. *She isn't going to forgive me for it, I knew it.*

"Take advantage of me?" she whispered.

"I won't do it again, I swear."

"Is that what this is about? Why you've been avoiding me all this time?"

Sam hunched over, preparing for a strike, but the blow never came.

"Sam." She stood and glided over to him. With a tender touch, she lifted his head. The flames of the fire licked up. Their eyes met, more than words passing between them.

Sam was more lightheaded than ever, but she was there, mere inches from his body. He reached out a trembling hand, and she took it, lacing her fingers through his and holding onto him fiercely. She looked up at him with those soft eyes, and her soft lips parted.

"I have been a fool," he said, mouth dry and cracking. He moistened his lips.

"No more a fool than I."

Gently, he wrapped an arm around her hips and pulled her in close, pressing her body up against his. Martha's eyes closed, and he leaned down.

Lips touched, and they melted into each other's arms.

19

New Walls

"What if they make it through, or what if they never even take the gate?" Evan paced with his hands behind his back, then went back to the book. "They're going to have the advantage of numbers and we have to negate it."

"We still fall back to the Keep, but we can harass them as they come." Sam pointed to the sketch, drawing a line down the new walls that he had suggested long ago. "As long as we have holes to shoot from, we stand a good chance."

"We'll have to reinforce the northern wall." Evan tried to think of every angle they might take. "It will bear the brunt of the attack."

"Agreed." It was the shallowest point on the Black River. Anywhere else would be either too deep or take too much time to build rafts. The Castle was well positioned to oversee it though.

"And you think you can finish the norther tower defenses?"

"Once we get the interior walls finished, I think so."

"Then we have a plan." Evan stopped pacing and joined him at the desk. He looked down at their overhead view, and a strong memory of Yand took him.

He had been too dense to see it before, too naïve. Evan shook his head. He learned his lesson, though, and now he was not going to make the same mistake twice.

"You'll have the support of the masons, I'll see to it. Bill might not like it, but there will be no excuses this time."

Sam was silent.

"What is it?" Evan asked. The faint smell of lunch hung in the air, a hearty stew and freshly baked rolls.

"Just something Bill said." Sam shook his head. "Never mind. It isn't worth mentioning. It will be a lot of work, and I can't see it being done before spring comes, or even summer."

"It will have to be sooner than that. Early spring will be the latest I expect the Belmarch to march." His muscles were still sore, but he would get a chance to limber them up after they were done. "We can't wait for spring to start, let alone wait for it to finish."

"We're up against time. The soldiers will have to work, too."

"You'll have them."

"It will take a miracle to survive, or an army," Sam said, putting his hands on the desk and leaning over the sketch.

"Since we don't have an army, let's hope for a miracle."

Sam traced the new walls. "What do you think happened to Rhys?"

The question caught him by surprise. "He made it to the capital and sent us help."

"That's what I thought too, but Silverthorn left before Rhys could have had the chance."

"Where did you hear that?"

"The soldiers. I've been talking to them. They left two months ago and had trouble in the snows."

Evan did the calculations in his head, thinking back to how many weeks ago Rhys had left. Sam was right. It couldn't have been him.

"It doesn't matter what happened to him." Evan shoved aside the fear that the thought brought with it, adding to the fuel of the nightmare. *I could use a drink.*

"You're probably right. I just hope he made it...to wherever he was going."

Evan leaned over and blew out the candle. They were done with it now, and habit forced him to conserve it. He smiled.

How differently he acted. Just a few weeks and months in brutal conditions and he was thinking of things like saving a candle.

"He's more tenacious than he looks, and he can handle himself." Evan glanced at his mother's letter. "And he'll need it in the King's Court. Never has there been a larger gathering of snakes and backstabbers."

Sam frowned. "You seem to have some experience with it."

"Experience?" Evan said through gritted teeth. "I was forced there every summer for the first few decades of my life. It was horrible, but I managed to sneak away at night and make things a little more interesting." His snarl turned into a more natural smile as he thought of the better times.

But then the shame came with it, and the smile faded.

"I can't say I'm jealous of your situation," Sam said. He stood, stretching his legs and arms. "You couldn't pay me enough to take it away from you."

"You wouldn't make a good court attendant. They're all so filled with themselves and desperate for power they'd do anything." Evan furrowed his brows, remembering some of the least desirable. "And I mean anything."

Silence grew between them. Voices, muffled by the distance and the door, drifted down the hallway. Then it was gone.

"Surviving might be a worse situation than the alternative," Sam said. "I hope..."

"Yes."

"Well, no use dwelling on it now. We've got a castle to fortify and an angry horde of Belmarch to prepare for." Sam bowed and gave him a proper salutation, and Evan dismissed him.

He shut the door with a gentle click as he left. Evan was alone once again.

Instead of dwelling on it, he picked up his sword and worked through the forms once, letting them flow through him until they had loosened his muscles and brought him to a short breath.

The next few days passed quickly. They made good progress on the modifications since the snow had stopped and began to melt.

Sam led a group out into the forest to pick up as much leaves and kindling as he could, and they piled some next to the workshop while the rest were dumped over the side of the north wall.

The walls were laid out, and the foundations dug into the softening ground. Everyone pitched in, despite their desire not to, and Evan saw to it that no man shirked by getting down in the mud himself and taking a turn.

After that, no one complained. Bit by bit, the forms began to take shape. Evan started to see how the walls would go up side by side.

And as he stood over it in the warming sun, water dripping from the eaves of the roofs, the hard knot in his stomach grew even harder.

"Don't be daunted by the size," Sam said, coming up from behind him. "Bill and the masons may not look it, but they can work when they have to. Now that they have some clear direction and a purpose, you'll see that it goes up quickly."

"I hope you're right," was all he could say in return. As he watched the progress, which seemed slow in comparison to what they needed, he wondered if he should call off the nightly training and focus all efforts on the construction.

He pondered it, thought about it, agonized over it, for hours that day. In the end he decided it was better to have a group of fighters ready and prepared than a few sets of walls.

They wouldn't be much good without the skills needed to survive.

So, Evan let the training continue, and attended when he could, working on his own forms when he tired of watching the others spar and train.

He thought about joining them, but knew he would outclass them and didn't want to embarrass any of them. Those lessons he had paid attention to and could see that Sam knew what he was teaching.

It roused his suspicion even more and became something of a thorn in his side. *Where did this man come from, and why is he so adept at fighting?*

Evan set Barger to find out as much as he could, but the servant came up empty-handed every night.

Then, one night, Barger came in with a hint of a smile on his face.

"What is it?" Evan asked. There was something good on the plates he carried, but he was more interested in what Barger had in his head.

"I've found something out about our friend, Sam Freeman."

20

THE ROAD AHEAD

"It's no good mi'Lord, the pass is too wet to get through." Raltone stared down at the quagmire of men and arms. Thick, brown mud covered every one of them up to their knees. His own steed, a great black stallion, shied away from the road below, backing up from the squishy grass. "We must turn back," Sable said at his left.

"General, what do you think?"

"I think we need to wait until it dries for us to get the baggage train through. If we don't, the men will starve."

"It could be a risk I'm willing to take." Raltone looked up to the mountains beyond, the pass rising to their blue base that was still frosted with white. A few more miles and they would be over it, a few days travel in good conditions.

"Turn back to the last dry encampment. We'll wait." Raltone turned his steed and kicked it into a trot, not waiting for the others to join. If he had to wait here, he might as well do it in style.

Winter still clung stubbornly to the mountains, even though the valleys were long ago melted and covered with new growth. It was always a risk, but he'd thought they could make it.

Sable caught up to him, bringing his own horse in line. Raltone noted that he almost came fully abreast.

"We could go around them to the west," Sable said. "It would take less time if we used it. We could catch them unaware."

"Since the failure of my previous men, I'm sure they are well aware we are coming." Raltone thought about it, then pulled up his short.

A sly smile crept across his face. "There is something you can do for me Sable."

Sable swallowed. "Yes, mi'Lord?"

Sam helped wrestle the stone the last few inches, sweat pouring down his back. It slid into place as they tipped it off the roller and sank into the mud at the bottom of the hole.

"There. Not the best conditions for building your wall, but it will have to do." Bill wiped off his hands, then walked back to the long row of masons dressing stone.

Sam leaned back to rest and catch his breath. The first of his improvements was in full swing now, a new set of walls that led from the gate up to the Keep.

They were no ordinary walls. Each was actually a set of walls, forming a hollow channel in the middle. This was going to be key to their use, once done.

And when the gate was breached, which he was planning on now, they would prove a nasty surprise for whoever came in.

When he had recovered, Sam walked back to the workshop. Trent and Kerien were working, with another small set of hands helping. Sam frowned at the young boy who kept his head down as he darted about the workshop.

"Almost done with this one, then we have a few more to go." Kerien patted his timber, a relatively short beam that would help tie the two walls together. They had enough lumber, but it was so green.

Sam didn't like using it like this, but they didn't have much choice.

It wouldn't play well with the stone, as wet as it was, and he wasn't sure how well it would hold up.

Would it shrink too much and pull the wall over prematurely? Or worse, right in the middle of an attack?

He hated the thought, envisioning an opening in their defenses and the enemy seizing on the advantage.

They wouldn't stand a chance.

"Good. Well done," Sam said. Kerien stopped what he was doing and swiveled around with wide eyes. Sam rubbed at a spot of mud on his trousers and walked to his workbench.

He wasn't sure why Kerien was giving him the look, but he let it pass and slumped onto his stool to recover. The stone was heavy and had taken a lot out of him, but he was grateful it was in. The rest of the wall would be built now, and none too soon.

Fresh air was bringing with it the warm smell of spring, and they had thrown the flaps of the workshop open to let it in. Sam breathed it in, grateful for the increase in temperature but wary of what it might bring.

The rivers were still swollen, fed with the snow melt high up in the north. It would protect them, for now, but come the end of spring it would die down and recede, leaving the river passable once again.

Trent was busy with his work, but once Sam recovered he went over to inspect. The cheeks of the tenons were smooth and fairly flat. Not perfect, but they didn't have time for that perfection. He checked them for square, and they were good enough.

"Better work on the sides, although you can clean up the shoulders more here."

"I thought about that but didn't have the time. Won't it be covered up in the wall?"

"Yes, but it has to be flat enough to seat properly. See where it waves here." Sam traced the center, which was bent out in a u shape. "That will stop the tenon from going all the way through. If you have to make a mistake, make sure the edges are the highest points." Sam walked Trent through some pointers, showing him a few different ways to make the cuts.

"Try one on the next few. Don't give up on it until you've gotten the hang of it. After that, if you prefer another way, do it."

"Thank you." Trent gave a little nod, then took up his chisel.

"You're welcome." Something about Trent's tone made him warm inside, like he had lighted a fire within him. This time, though, it was good.

He wanted to tell someone about it, but then realized that he didn't have anyone to tell. Martha wouldn't look at him it seemed, let alone give him the time of day to talk to him.

"Go ahead and keep working." The feeling inside was suppressed, and Sam moved on to Kerien.

His work was solid, but not perfect. Sam complimented him on it, and Kerien gave him another one of those looks.

"What's gotten into you?" he asked.

"What do you mean?"

"You aren't insulting me, or telling me everything I do is wrong."

That stung a little. "I don't think that is fair," Sam said, crossing his arms. "You have always had potential in there somewhere, and I'm glad it's coming out. That's it."

Part of him remembered Ned and the advice he had given him, how he opened his eyes to what was right in front of him. Another part of him knew he was down to two carpenters, and there was a lot of work still to go on the castle. He was going to need all the help he could get, and if it meant making them feel a little better, he would do it.

"You're just different, that's all I'm saying." Kerien returned to his work. "Not that I want you to go back."

Sam snorted. "Give me enough excuses and I'll leave in a heartbeat."

Kerien smiled, but his pace of work picked up.

Jospeh, the youngest addition to the crew, was busy sweeping up, and Sam stopped him, kneeling down to see him better eye to eye.

"How is your mother?"

"Good."

"Getting enough to eat?" Joseph nodded. "Good." Sam mussed his hair. "Make sure you get into all the corners. Collect everything, we're going to need it for later." He had plans for this.

Joseph nodded, and went back to sweeping. Sam watched him, wondering what it would be like to have a child. The thought of it, and who he might like to have one with, made his cheeks flush and he turned away quickly back to his own work.

No time to think about foolish thoughts like that.

Sam threw himself into his work, keeping going night and day. He tried to get as much done as he could, but the days seemed to fly by without stopping.

Logs rolled into the courtyard and into the workshop faster than they could process them. The resulting timbers were sucked up almost as quickly as they touched the finished pile, straight into the wall that was going up faster than they could keep up.

Bill was driving the masons now, with Evan standing over his back, watching almost every waking second.

Time in the workshop was split up by meals and training, with a few hours to sleep each night, but Sam and the others worked by torchlight far into the night.

The days went by. The work started taking its toll. Sam was sleeping less and less, dreaming up new defenses and different ideas of what could be done to strengthen their position.

Most of it he discarded. Some of it was good enough to take to Duke Hornblood, and a few of those were debated and implemented.

If the Belmarch were coming back, they would be met with some nasty surprises.

He was so caught up in his work he almost forgot about Martha, or meant to. He would see her almost every meal and think about her every night before he went to bed replaying that scene over and over in his head.

By the time he drifted off to sleep he wanted to pull his hair out in shame. When he woke up the next morning he would always resolve to find a way to make it up to her, to make it right somehow.

And every day he ended the day having not done so. But he felt that there was no one to confide in, no one he could talk to about it.

Ned was gone, and he wasn't comfortable talking to Dale about it, if he could find the time. Dale was more overworked than he was, constantly working to repair the tools of both the masons and their own, in addition to all the other work that demanded iron around the castle.

They hadn't gotten a new shipment of ore with the last supply, so Dale was forced to have his apprentices scrounge and scrape up anything they could. Nails from old boxes in the basement, old horse shoes stuck in the mud revealed by the warming weather, and he was forced to do most of the work himself.

Sam commiserated with him from time to time over a meal, but by the time it was over they were both whisked off to their respective duties and never had time to breathe.

All of this was in addition to training the men in combat and war fighting. That took almost all his energy alone, and Sam was beginning to tire of it. He started snapping at anyone who complained too much, or didn't do as he said quick enough.

Men were starting to avoid him, to shy away from him, but he was so tired he didn't care much.

There was something far more important on his mind, and something far more pressing to deal with.

He was feeling the effects, though, his movements becoming sluggish after a few weeks straight of the intense schedule. Sam kept telling himself it wasn't happening, that he was just fine, even though he was making more and more mistakes.

Finally, it caught up to him at one evening dinner, when he fell asleep and drenched himself in the evening stew. That woke him up faster than anything else.

"Sam, we need to get you to bed." Martha was at his side somehow. He hadn't seen her come over. The stew dripped off his face and soaked the front of him. She tugged at his arm.

"I'm fine. Leave me be." He tried to pull his arm away, but she kept a hold of it with a surprisingly strong grip. "There is more to do."

"And there will be more to do tomorrow. Come on, up with you." She nodded to Kerien at his side, who helped him to his feet.

Sam blinked away the sleep and told them he was fine to walk. Everyone in the great hall was watching him, silent over the sound of fire at the far end of the room. Sam felt it, but he was too tired to feel shame.

"Go, I've got him," Martha said when they were in the hall.

"Are you sure?" Kerien asked.

"My legs work fine," Sam said. "And I'm right here, you know."

"He might need some help down the stairs." Kerien had bags under his eyes too.

"Go get your dinner," Martha said, and shooed him off. She wiped down Sam's front with a handkerchief as Kerien left.

"Thank you for your help, but I can manage from here."

Martha stared up at him through narrowed eyes, a hand on her hip. "No, you don't, Sam Freeman. I know what you're going to do the moment I'm out of sight."

21

MOVEMENT

Evan watched from afar as the castle defenses took shape. The work he had done was long over, but it had its intended effect.

And he was sure his father wouldn't have approved of his actions, but that was only at the back of his mind. Even now, he thought of the lessons Yand had taught him, of how to treat those below you with respect.

Evan found himself outside, watching the work progress, as the warm, spring sun shone down and glinted off the chisels of the masons. Hammer blows rung out, a simple melody that echoed around the courtyard and bounced back and forth. Small shoots of green were coming up in the less heavily trafficked areas of the yard, and at the base of the walls, a hopeful reminder of the season to come.

Nearly all the snow had melted, except the most stubbornly deep drifts in the shade, and the last snowfall had been weeks ago. That made Evan think of the lands to the north, and how they too would be thawing and melting.

Feet squished through the resulting mud, a thick, brown paste that seemed to be everywhere and get into everything. Long streaks of it were trailed into the Keep, much to the chagrin of the ladies, and it was ever present.

"It's coming along, isn't it?" Sam stepped up beside him, stopping to rest before he took another load of beams to the half-finished walls. They had most of the lower courses complete, laid out in the straight lines that would eventually be above their heads, and it was clear what it would look like at this point.

"You look horrible," Evan said, looking the man over.

"Thanks," he said dryly. His hair was unkempt and looked like it hadn't been cared for in weeks, and his eyes were red and bloodshot. "If you can imagine, it was worse yesterday."

"I heard about that."

"Ah." Sam licked his lips but kept his eyes on the masons. Bill was keeping them working, and in line, and they seemed to be working efficiently. The horses that Silverthorn had left were essential to keep the rock flowing from the quarry now that they had run out of what had been stored within the walls.

"I would like to rest more, but..."

Evan shook his head. "Say no more." He, too, had been up countless hours. It was difficult to sleep. "With the sword hanging over your head, it is hard to sleep."

Sam nodded.

"On the other hand, the training seems to be going well. I've heard the soldiers remark on the improvement in the few weeks they've been here," Evan said, watching for a reaction.

He didn't get one. Sam only seemed to stew in his thoughts. *Should I reveal it now?*

"If you'll excuse me, Your Highness?"

Evan nodded, and Sam picked up his pair of beams, setting off for the far end of the wall. He watched from afar, leaning against the side of the Keep in the sun.

Trent joined Sam with another pair after a few minutes, and together they pulled them up the nearly complete wall. The masons had left notches at the top, and the two men made some final adjustments to the beams before dropping them into this space and hammering them home with an oversized mallet. Evan had seen this happen more than a few times and knew that the masons would come behind and lay the final few courses on top to complete the wall, tying them together.

That left a space wide enough for a man to draw an arrow in, both to the interior path that led directly from the gate to the Keep, and the courtyard on either side.

Evan still wasn't sure it would work well, but he had to trust Sam's instinct. From what he knew about him now it would be a good idea to do so.

Eventually the noon bell rang, and Evan reluctantly left the warm, sunny courtyard to retreat back into the Keep for the meal.

It was nothing special, drawn from the supplies that had been brought up, but included some berries that a few foraging parties had stumbled across in the wood. They were red and sweet, a type of strawberry that grew in the forest, and complemented the fresh bread that the women had prepared.

Whoever made it knew what they were doing, for day after day it came out light and fluffy on the outside with a wonderfully crisp crust on the outside. It was good enough by itself, which was good because their supplies of butter and cheese had run out. Anything that remained was carefully locked away in the cellar in the emergency rations.

Evan distasted even the thought of it. A whole cellar set aside to feed the castle in the event of another siege. He wasn't sure what they would do if it came to that, but was certain that the enemy army coming would have no patience for it.

And that was what scared him the most.

They would have the advantage of numbers, not some small raiding party like the last one. He would do the same in the

Belmarch leader's place, and he hated that there was nothing he could do about it.

But he had sent his message south with Silverthorn, to be delivered to his father, if he still lived.

That brought a grimace to Evan's face, so much so that Barger asked about it as he was clearing away the remains of his lunch.

"I'm not ready."

"Ready for what, Your Highness?" Barger worked smoothly and methodically.

"To be Archduke." Evan stood up, irritated at the thought of it, and started pacing around his room. The old thirst returned to him, and Barger seemed to notice.

"I understand. I was not prepared to come here, and yet the task came to me."

"You didn't have much choice, did you?"

"I did have a choice."

Evan froze. That wasn't something he had ever thought about, and he turned back to Barger. "What?"

"I was offered a different position. One with less...honor and opportunity for advancement. However, it was tempting in its own right."

"Someone...gave you the chance to not come here with me?"

"Yes."

"And you didn't take it?" Evan drilled into him with his eyes.

"After how I treated you all those years?"

He was ashamed of it, and it leaked into his voice. His old self had been horrible, hadn't even known Barger's name or even noticed him.

"Correct."

"Why?"

Barger's lips pursed ever so slightly. "That is a question I asked myself for a while," he said softly, careful with his words.

"I won't take offense," Evan promised. He might not have been the best master, but he could make up for it now if just to hear Barger out.

"I made a promise." Evan wanted to urge him on, but he saw that the man was thinking, considering what to say next, and he waited until he continued. "To Captain Yand. When I was younger, he made me make a promise to take care of you when he was gone. He said you needed solid men around you to keep you out of trouble."

Despite the sadness that the words stirred in him, Evan couldn't help but feel a small smile creep onto his face. "Well, he was right, wasn't he?"

Barger's face reflected the smile. It improved the man's appearance, and Evan realized it might have been the first time he had ever seen it. "He was right, Your Highness. Although, I think he would have recognized the man you are as who he thought you would be."

"I'm a long way from that," Evan said, a hint of sadness coming back into his voice. Yand had always treated him better than he deserved, always expected him to be a better man than he was.

The loss pained him even more. Evan wished he could take Yand back to the Hornwood and bury him as he deserved. He was better than the shallow grave he'd been given.

At that moment, Evan resolved to do it. "When we get out of this I'm going to lay Yand to rest as he should be."

Barger nodded, sensing his sadness. "I'll take my leave, Your Highness, and take these back to the kitchens."

Evan nodded and bid the servant a good day. The pressure hadn't been relieved, but it had helped to share a smile. Evan never expected it would have, and then realized how fond he had grown of Barger.

The man has been with me for years. How had the servant found his way into the Duke's service? Evan couldn't remember, for that matter, he couldn't remember selecting any of his servants.

His mother? That would be the most logical choice. She always had a keen eye for servants, who was the best and where to place them. Her lady-in-waiting had been at her side for decades, ever since she had married his father or longer, or so he heard.

How does she do it? Evan wondered as he went through his afternoon training, sliding into the forms that came easier and easier every day. They were starting to flow like water now. He entered one, and the motions rippled and cascaded over his body, then he was done and out the other side, breathing deep with his sword still outstretched.

With little else to do, Evan finished another set and then read through another book on warfare. The new books caught his eye as he finished, and he took one out with him to the wall, intending to watch the progress.

The rivers were raging, flooded with the melting snow farther to the north, each lapping at and spilling out of its banks. Evan guessed they had to be five feet higher than normal, and a hearty moat to keep out any enemies.

He dwelled on what it meant to set the castle here, right at the most defensible position between Chathem and Belmarch. Whoever had chosen the spot had been wise, with the rocky shoreline a good foundation to build upon.

There were no other bridge between the two countries. If they had they had long ago been destroyed in the generations of fighting that had been exchanged, the Belmarch almost always the assessor.

He examined the other side, just as covered in trees, that extended out and up to a mountain range off in the distance. Its craggy peaks pierced the green tops of the trees, then rose to white caps that looked difficult to traverse, a perfect wall to keep out any that tried to invade Belmarch. Evan suspected those mountains and the hard packed earth beyond them were why the Belmarch always desired Chathem lands. All that came out of them was metal and dust, little in the way of food and sustenance.

However, Chathem was a land rich in soil, good for growing crops and timber. He imagined he would desire them if he were in the Belmarch's place, not that it excused their blood-thirsty actions.

He blinked. Evan found that time had gotten away from him in his thoughts. The spring wind had died down, and with it the warmth. A chill was on the air, even though most of the land surrounding the castle was starting to turn green. Shoots of grass poked up through the tiny bits of snow still left in the shadows and blossomed everywhere else.

Behind him, the work had progressed. It looked like the carpenters had put up another few beams, and the masons were finishing the last few courses of the stone beneath the connectors. Small windows looked out over the courtyard, big enough to shoot an arrow through but a challenge to try to shoot back in.

Forms passed through the two walls, masons carrying stone most likely, but it was difficult to see them from this far away on the wall. Evan examined the new defenses, thinking as he would if he were the enemy.

The Keep was solid and well built, designed and construct-ed with one entrance that was now flanked by two walls. Going through the side might be a tactic they might take, but Evan wouldn't. The door looked to be the softest spot.

And now it was hardened with extra fortifications. Evan hoped that it would be enough, but after the siege he wasn't sure. That hadn't been a whole army.

Evan looked back to Belmarch, squinting in the late afternoon sun. Something about it didn't feel right.

Out of the corner of his eye, he saw movement on the opposite bank. Evan bolted upright and stared into the trees at the spot, waiting for movement again.

He didn't have to wait long.

22

A Pledge and Oath

Then it was gone. Evan thought it might be a mistake, a strange daydream, because no matter how hard he looked he couldn't make out that form again.

The shape of a man, brief and darkened in the shadow of the trees, but a man nonetheless.

A chill ran down Evan's back, and the ramifications hit him like a rock. He glanced back to the new fortifications, and the new surprises they had in store.

Soldiers and workers were toiling, moving rock and wood and metal as fast as they could, but it wouldn't be enough. They weren't finished, they weren't ready.

But it seemed that time was up. After the long days of preparation, the hard work that had gone into this already. It was too late to do any more.

There was another sentry on the wall, farther down to the west, and Evan approached. "What did you see?"

The man clutched at his spear. Evan had seen him working rock often, a mason. He looked down. "I thought I saw..."

"A person, on the other side of the river?"

The man nodded. Evan breathed deep, the smell of spring fresh in the air, a contrast to what he was feeling deep inside. "I saw it too."

"It wasn't real, was it?"

Evan looked back across the river. It was quiet. "Keep a close eye on that bank. If you see anything else, don't hesitate to raise the alarm." Evan clapped the man on the back. "Stand firm. These walls were well built, and thick. They will stand."

He wondered how often his father had spoken words he wanted to feel but didn't. It didn't feel good, but he believed them, or at least he told himself that.

The stone walls were thick and firm beneath his feet, more than just a few inches wide, and had already withstood a beating.

But there was so much of it, and too few defenders to properly defend it. Not for the first time Evan wondered why they had made it so big, but put it out of his mind.

He left the sentry and went to the northern tower, climbing the steep, winding stairs around the circular tower to the top where he could get the best view.

Another sentry was there, watching Belmarch. "Have you seen anything?"

The man started and whirled around to face him. "No, Your Highness," he stammered.

Evan squinted and looked as far as he could into Belmarch. No smoke, no fires, not even a cloud of dust, but since it had been so wet he didn't think there would have been. It was quiet, empty. Not even a flock of birds flew there.

Perhaps it was a figment of his imagination, but then why had the other man reported the same thing?

Evan kept calm, trying to not let the raging emotions inside him show, and left after an appropriate amount of time. His footsteps rang on the stone stairs as he descended, his heart pounding in his ears.

He went first to the guardhouse, finding Mathew and telling him to double the guard.

"Double, Your Highness?" Mathew asked.

"And prepare the arms for distribution."

"You know something then." Mathew's brows furrowed.

"Do as I say, but do it quietly. No need for alarm yet, just caution."

Mathew saluted. Levitus was next, and Evan found him working with the other soldiers hauling rock. Evan pulled him off to the side and told him what he'd seen.

"We will be ready, Your Highness." Levitus bowed in obedience, unfazed by his words. Solidly built, he seemed to exhibit that in every aspect of his nature. "I will get the men ready now."

"No, keep them working." They were at the top course. Evan wasn't sure how critical it was. "Might as well use the time we have."

The dinner bell rang then, interrupting his plans. Evan dismissed Levitus but told him to send a messenger for Sam to meet him in his study. A light drizzle from blue clouds above dripped down, soaking him. He smelled rain in the air as soon as he realized what was happening and hurried back inside.

Dinner was waiting for him when he arrived, and he stripped his coat to dry by the fire. Evan glanced at the food but was so consumed with worry that he couldn't touch it, no matter how tempting it looked. Venison on a bed of potatoes.

Instead, he paced round the room until Sam knocked on the door and entered at his command.

"You wanted to see me, Your Highness?"

Evan bade him to sit, but continued pacing.

"I'm afraid were' out of time." Evan again recounted the story, bringing a thundercloud to Sam's face.

"We knew they would come," Sam said, face taut. "I wish we had more time."

"As do we all, but will what we have work?"

"No." Sam slowly shook his head. "Bill needs to set that final course for it to work as intended."

"How long will it take?"

"Another day or two, maybe longer. He wasn't sure the last time I asked him and I was so caught up in my own work." Sam spread his hands. "We needed the arrows, and we only have four of us."

Evan stopped and spun on his heel to face him. "Have you had anything to eat?"

Sam shook his head.

"Then take mine. Go ahead, I can't eat it."

Sam looked exhausted, even after getting some rest. Evan suspected he had been up, despite his desire that he sleep more. "You haven't been sleeping well?"

Sam crossed his arms and looked at the food.

"Go on, have it. It will be thrown away if you don't."

At last, and with great reluctance, Sam picked up the silver fork and started to eat.

"I'm having nightmares. It's hard to sleep."

The man was almost twice his age, or he looked like it. Evan saw something in his eyes, a hint of the past life that he kept locked away.

"I'm going to need fighting men, Sam." Evan clasped his hands behind his back, and spoke barely above a whisper. "I don't know why you want to hide your past from us, or what you feel you did that was so bad, but the time for building has come and gone. I need a destroyer."

Sam's face flashed, a myriad of emotions playing over it. "I don't think you understand what you ask of me."

"I understand completely. It isn't just our lives at stake here. If we don't hold this castle, you know where the Belmarch will go, and what they will do. Our lives will be forfeit if we can't find the will to stand up and fight." Evan saw that he was too conflicted, like so many men that were drinking in the taverns. Hard lives they wanted to escape, like the lonely one he wanted to leave. "I'm not asking you to do this for me. I'm asking you to do this for them."

Evan pointed beyond his door. "For the ones who have already sacrificed their lives. For the ones that survived. The children that will become young men and women, the families that would be torn to shreds if we didn't stop them. The friends you hold dear, the men you work beside and sweat beside and bleed beside. I'm asking you to do this for them, not for me."

"There is a beast within me," Sam said, his face finally calming. He looked peaceful. "A monster that consumes and destroys. It isn't what I did that I'm running from." His eyes flashed to Evan's. "It's who I am."

There was a danger lurking there, not hidden well. Evan wanted to draw back, suddenly afraid of this man sitting before him, but he ignored it. He had confronted men who had wanted to take his life and lived to tell the tale.

"Who are you, then?"

Sam drew back his head in surprise and blinked.

"Are you not Sam Freeman? Master of the carpenters at Hornblood Castle, Overseer, trainer, lover?"

That last got to him, and Sam's mouth parted. The danger in his eyes was gone, replaced with embarrassment.

"Who you are is not who you were." Evan held out a hand. "It is not who you have to be."

Sam considered his hand, agitated and fidgeting, a strange condition for Evan to see him in.

Finally, after what seemed like minutes, he stood and took his hand. His grip was powerful, hard and firm, but his hand was warm.

"Tell me, if I fight for you, what will happen?" Sam looked deep into Evan's eyes. "Will you be the man who came here?" Something was bubbling between them, and Evan wasn't sure if it was a test or something else.

"No. That man is gone, drowned in his own ego."

"Then we will go as two men of our own, not what we were, and fight together," Sam said.

"Together." Evan nodded.

"And will you be the Duke of Hornblood?"

"I will."

Sam smiled then. The tension that had been building between them evaporated.

"Then I will go, make as much progress with what little time we can, and live up to what you expect."

Evan watched him go, then stopped him as he opened the door. "The ending."

"What?"

"Sometimes the endings don't always turn out right."

Sam turned back. "I'm not sure I understand."

"In the books." Evan went to his desk and picked one up. "Most turn out happy in the end, but not all."

Sam gave him a half smile, then left.

Evan slumped into the chair by the fire, letting the tension flow from his body and forcing it to relax. They might not have much time, but this was going to be his last peaceful night in a long time, of that he was certain.

Raltone looked down on the castle, the cold night wind rustling his hair and stinging his cheeks.

He wanted it burned. It was an affront to him and his people. "For too long we've been seen as backward, unable to take care of ourselves, and savages. That ends now."

A murmur ran through the group behind him. His horse whinnied and Raltone pulled up the reins, backing it up from the edge of the mountain.

Behind him his troops flowed through the still-soggy pass. "How long until they are through?"

"About five more hours mi'Lord and everyone and everything will be on the other side," Granb said.

"I was asking Sable."

Granb frowned, then hid it and bowed. He pulled back.

Sable looked uncomfortable, sickly, but he pulled up. "He speaks the truth. They should be over tonight while the darkness still holds."

"I want no fires, not a hint given away. Not even a scout." He got no response and stopped staring at the fires through the windows of the castle to turn back.

Both Granb and Sable shifted in their saddles.

"What is it?" His voice carried a hint of warning.

"We had sent a scout already, mi'Lord," Granb said after a long, uncomfortable silence.

"Who gave that order?" He was barely whispering, and both of them leaned forward. Neither answered at first. "Shall I have both of you removed and imprisoned?"

"It was I," Sable said, looking down. "I had no idea that wasn't what you wanted, mi'Lord. I would not have done it."

Raltone frowned as he stammered. "When we get there, I want you to lead the attack personally. From the front."

Sable's eyes widened, but he swallowed and wisely kept his mouth shut. Raltone took one last look while they had the advantage of elevation, scanning the swollen river for any sign of stopping, then turned his steed back down the slope and onto the narrow path.

The others followed, and they descended the mountain. As they did the castle was obstructed by the trees, but inside Raltone was starting to feel the excitement build.

The entire land of Chathem lay before him, and with the eastern raiders paid off to invade they wouldn't be prepared for attack.

The time was finally right for him to claim what was rightfully theirs.

23

ALL IS WELL

Evan wiped the sweat from his brow and paused to catch his breath. Men kept moving, carrying stone from the masons down below up to the wall above in the torchlight.

The night had a warmth to it, the hint of spring in full bloom. Evan squinted against the darkness, trying to see how much longer they had to go.

He couldn't make it out, and ended up giving up until he could get back to the top himself. His coat had been shed long ago, like the others, his body warm enough from the work.

Evan went back to the line, waiting to get another block. He didn't have long to wait, the masons were carving at a furious rate. Soon they handed him a roughly shaped stone, good enough to get to the top, where Bill was directing the final finishing and placement.

The stone was large, and heavy, and weighed him down, but Evan went to the makeshift ladder and tied it to the rope. With a quick jerk he signaled the men at the top and mounted the ladder, racing to get up it before the stone was off the ground.

Two men heaved at the rope, exhaustion straining their muscles and showing in their face, and he grabbed onto the rough, fibrous rope and helped. In a few pulls it was at the top, and Evan regained his load and walked carefully across the stone wall down to the end.

"Put it here," Bill said, pointing beside him, then turned, "Your Highness," he added, belatedly and with a toothy smile.

Evan let the rock drop into place. It sank into the prepared mortar, which dripped out the sides and flowed down the wall. He stepped back to let Bill examine it. "Good enough without dressing, on to the next one." A mason followed him, scooping out more mortar from his reed bag and working it between his stone and the ones next to it to fill the gaps. He wasn't thorough, but pushed with his trowel until most of the gap disappeared.

"How long do you need?" Evan asked, coming up behind Bill.

Bill squinted, then licked his thumb before holding it up before him. "A few days and we'd have it finished at this rate."

"Is there any way to go faster?"

"Yes," Bill said, staring at him. "Give me more masons."

"That's the one thing I can't make."

"One?" Bill smiled, but Evan wasn't concerned at it, and even had to smile back. Bill was like many men he had wasted nights with drinking and carousing, and had a familiar spirit that resonated with Evan.

He wasn't sure why, given the man's past and the things he had done, or was accused of at least. For the moment, Evan wasn't concerned. He might need men who were prone to violence and was glad it wasn't going to be directed toward him for a change.

"You being out here has helped," Bill said, pausing to sit and rest. "I have to give you credit for it, and I'm not sure I would have believed it had someone told me you'd be willing to work alongside us a few weeks ago."

"We all have our...quirks, don't we?" Evan joined him, looking up at the clouds that drifted over the face of a nearly full moon. The smell of wildflowers was in the air, but the sound of the river had lessened.

Only in the moment of peace did he notice it. The one thing that stood between them and Belmarch, and it was dying down like it wanted to invade.

Soon it would trickle to a stream as the majority of the Venti shifted to the Golden River and open up its path to man and beast. Evan wished its bottom would stay mud, that it would suck at their feet and drag them down, but knew it was a useless hope.

In a few days it would practically be a road to an army, with them sitting in a castle right at the end of it, flat and ready to be plucked like a goose.

"Back to work. You've had enough rest," Evan said, rising to his feet. Bill joined him, with grumbling that he couldn't hear.

Evan spent the next few hours helping until Bill called an end to the shift for everyone to get rest. He stayed for a few more rounds of stone hauling, then was too tired to go any further and slipped away to his bed.

It welcomed him like a warm glove and, before he could even dream, the morning light woke him again.

Evan sat up and rubbed the sleep from his eyes. Someone knocked at his door and through a yawn, he invited them in.

Barger walked through carrying a tray of food. "Good morning, Your Highness. I thought you might like something to eat."

Evan's stomach grumbled. It had been a while since he had eaten dinner the night before. "How long did I sleep?"

"Not long past breakfast, only a few hours."

Evan cursed and threw back the covers. He sprang out of bed onto the cold floor and started to dress. "Why didn't you wake me?"

"You needed the sleep, and it's quiet outside." Barger tended the fire, adding another log onto the banked ashes.

"You mean..."

"All is well."

"For now," Evan said, but inside he was elated. Another day, more work done. Sam and the carpenters were working on arrow shafts, and Dale was finishing as many heads as he could. They could sharpen the tips in a bind, but this was good news.

His mind was abuzz with thoughts, what they had to do, where they had to build, and Barger had to remind him to eat once the fire had begun to lick into flames at the fireplace.

Barely chewing, Evan gulped down his food. He wasn't sure what it was, but he had dressed and was out the door in less time than it took Barger to get the fire going and collect his dishes.

The sounds of construction grew louder the closer he got to the exit of the Keep. Hammers were ringing on chisels, and men were shouting and talking. There was little laughing, there wasn't enough time for anyone to get distracted that way.

Evan realized he'd forgotten a coat at the entrance door, but pushed it open anyway. It was warm outside, almost too warm for so early in spring, but he welcomed the feeling on his skin and would have breathed deep if he weren't so worried.

He went up the ladder and straight to the northern wall, watching Belmarch for any signs of the enemy. It was quiet, but Mathew was there too, watching.

"Good morning, Your Highness."

Evan gave a quick greeting. "What have you seen?"

"Nothing. It is quiet."

Evan breathed a sigh of relief. "Good."

"No, it's too quiet." Mathew looked to the other side of the river, staring intently into the forest. "Not a hint of wildlife, and no bird all morning."

The dread that had been reduced as soon as he saw Belmarch quiet started to grow again, and Evan reached for his sword, wrapping a hand around the hilt for reassurance. The cool of the leather felt good, solid.

"What are they waiting for?" Evan whispered, mostly to himself. Mathew had been stiff, and Evan wondered why.

Now, he knew. He felt it too, the keen edge that his body was prepared for something. Without knowing what it was his body was ready.

"Night," Mathew whispered. "They're waiting for nightfall."

In darkness they can hide. "Of course. Then we shall give them a night they will remember, won't we?"

Evan sat at his table, staring up at the Hornblood crest hanging over his desk. The sunlight was still coming in through the window, but it had turned a vibrant shade of red.

There were many things on his mind, and it seemed like a whirlwind. Was his father still alive? What was his mother doing? Would there be reinforcements sent as he'd asked?

He closed his eyes and put his head in his hands. He wished Yand were still here, a guiding hand and a wise counsel. He wished Silverthorn was still here, a fighter and a leader that would put everything right and make sure he knew what to do.

A part of him even wished his father were here, to take away this burden and lead the defenders how they should be led. He was realizing how much burden the Archduke had, and how it must make him do things he did not want to do.

Evan looked up, realizing the old hatred had been relegated to something far smaller than it was. It was still there, and he imagined it always would be, but he held something else bigger.

Respect.

Respect for what decisions his father had to make, for the actions he had to take to keep his family safe and his subjects protected. Evan had thought him cold and distant, but realized why he had been that way.

It was not an easy burden to bear.

A soft knock at the door disturbed him. Barger came in, as requested, but without a sound. There was too much heaviness in the air for words.

Evan stood and walked to the center of the room. Barger brought him his armor, piece by piece, and helped him put it on. Each added more weight to his body, but Evan took it in stride.

He took the helmet last, but did not put it on. It was cold on his fingers, a decorative Tree of Everlong worked into the crown. The roots traveled down the side of the helmet, a reminder of who was the root of the Hornbloods.

The last of the light was dying, and twilight was upon them. Barger stepped back, waiting as straight as an arrow, and Evan nodded to him.

He went out into the courtyard where the others had assembled under the cover of darkness. They were quiet, but ready for a fight.

Evan was the last to join. All eyes turned to him as he stepped into the yard. He glanced up at the wall.

Only two sentries walked it, watching in the night. Two, when there should have been more for an invading army on the horizon.

If they knew the army was there, that is.

Now was not a time for telling the enemy they knew they were coming, despite what he would rather have.

Evan turned back to the waiting group and examined their faces in the fast fading light.

Some were too young, some were too old. All of them were scared. He saw it in their eyes, felt it in their gaze. He felt it in his own heart, beating loudly in his chest, constricted by his breastplate.

"For Chathem." His words were merely a whisper, "and the defenders of Hornblood Castle."

His father would have made a bigger speech, a grander speech. One that would inspire them to fight harder than they ever could. He had to settle for the only words he knew to say, and to hope that they would be enough.

But as he looked out, and as the light faded, he thought he saw some ease to their fear. He didn't feel it himself. His hands trembled.

But he was going to have to lead despite it.

And then the sentry on the wall screamed out in pain.

Evan turned, careful to stay calm, as the others shied back. Sam stepped up beside him, and he was glad to have someone, anyone, there.

He froze. The man's scream cut off into a gurgle, then a death rattle. Something was up on the wall, a shadow against the moonlight.

His heart beat louder, faster. It was not an ordinary man, but worse.

24

A Feast for Vultures

"Archers!" Evan pulled out his sword. By the time he could point it at the figure, twangs from behind him were sounding, the whistle of arrows flying overhead close behind.

The figure moved. Arrow flew past where it had just been and over the wall, harmlessly sailing by it.

Evan blinked. It had moved so fast he couldn't believe it, but there it was again. Only this time it wasn't moving out of the way.

It jumped off the wall, charging straight for them, straight for him, a blade glinting in the moonlight like a silver crescent streaking through the air.

Evan had no time to react, no time to think, but somehow his body moved to meet it. He brought his sword up and to the right, and it connected with the sword.

His hand almost spun back as the force of the monster knocked away his sword.

No, it can't be. Whatever it was didn't expect such power and jumped back.

But it was too late. Evan had seen it in the torchlight and had been overcome by fear.

An arrow flew by his ear. This time, it found its mark in the chest of the man-shaped monster.

It looked down and growled, then reached up a hairy claw and snapped the arrow in two. Black blood oozed from the wound, but it didn't seem to notice any more than that.

Men gasped behind him. Some cursed. Prayers were said, cries to gods that went up into the night sky.

The words shook him from his shock, and Evan emerged as if from a dream. The monster was moving again, coming for him, and he slipped into the forms, letting his body take over.

He ducked. The long, sinister blade swept over him, missing by an inch.

Planting his foot, he shoved forward with a thrust. All his strength went into it.

And his blade found flesh.

The thing roared, deafening him and almost driving him back by the sound alone. A sickly vomit smell washed over him, laden with death and decay, and the monster's fangs dripped with the blood of his victim.

It reached down, lightning fast, but Evan was already moving, setting his sword against its hamstring and pulling as he dove to the side.

He wasn't fast enough. It clipped his shoulder, knocking him off balanced, and he hit the ground hard.

Before he could get up the thing roared again. There was shouting now, a din of chaos. Arrows were flying.

His right shoulder was hurting, but Evan rose and turned to face it. Sam was holding it at bay with his spear while the others peppered it with arrow and strikes.

One man darted in with a sword, but the monster swatted him away. He flew up in the air and crumpled a dozen feet from where he'd started.

Evan ignored the blood pounding in his ears and his heart pounding in his chest. He couldn't wait for it to kill more.

He charged it, attacking with a vicious downward cut, but it was met with a counter.

The force of the monster's blade shook through his arm, rising almost to his head.

Evan pulled back, then tried again. Sam struck with the spear, distracting the monster, giving him enough of an opening to duck underneath it.

There was no time to wear it out, and Evan saw only one option. He struck at the unprotected neck, drawing a long line along it.

The monster roared again and stepped back to clutch at his neck. It was too much and too long, and it toppled backward.

Evan stopped, leaning on his sword to watch.

But he couldn't believe his eyes again. There, in a pool of its own blood, the body...changed.

"What is it?" someone asked.

"Devilry!" cried another. A murmur ran through the men.

All that was left of it was a dead man, sunken and shrunk, no sign of life.

Evan walked to it with a trembling hand, reaching out to touch it.

It was solid, no ghost, but there was no strength in those arms.

"Whatever it was, we killed it," he said.

"We can't face an army of those." Bill strode into the firelight. "The Belmarch have discovered evil powers. They've changed themselves to demons."

"We do not need to face an army of them," Sam said. He was farther back, his face obscured in the shadows. Whispers ran through the group.

Evan's shoulder was hurting more. He tried to look at it but couldn't see much under his armor. There was no blood.

"Everyone to the wall. They will know that we won't be caught unaware."

They hesitated, but he turned and strode to the wall. He took the steps two at a time and found his place between two merlons.

The river was talking, not in the roar that he had hoped for in the rush of water that would keep it unpassable, but in a lighter hush.

Even in the night he knew it was possible to cross. Boulders that were near the bottom shone white as the water parted around them.

But there was no army crossing. Yet.

Levitus was shouting at the defenders, berating them for their fear.

Fear was great within him, though, and he kept replaying the fight in his head. It felt like it had gone on for so long, but he knew it was only moments.

Someone came up beside him.

"How do you know?" Evan asked.

"Whatever drove that man to do what he did, it was beyond painful to his body," Sam said. The dead man's face flashed in Evan's mind, the mouth twisted and contorted, the eyes wide in horror. "Even if they do have some ancient power, not all of them will be willing to use it. They are just as superstitious and suspicious of powers like that as we are."

"But we have no counter to it." Evan shuddered to think of hundreds of them climbing the walls, and he leaned over the side to check. They were empty. "There are two men dead to one, and there would have been more if we had to face them on our own."

Sam stared out over the river, then his hand tightened on his spear. "They come." As men filed by behind him, horns sounded across the river.

Evan looked to the tree line, just in time to see it stir.

"Bows at the ready," he called. The order went down the line, and arrows rattled. Those that had not strung them did so now.

Figures emerged from the shadows of the forest. What looked like the entire tree line moved out now, and men approached the shore.

The army of the Belmarch had come.

Evan started counting, but soon gave up as dozens turned into hundreds. They could not stand up against this many.

But if they did not, then he had no doubt they would kill and murder. Dread turned into outright fear, and only his hand on the merlon beside him held him up.

"There are so many," someone said.

"We could flee," another said.

"There will be no escape," Sam said, raising his voice. "They will come after you and chase you down. They would kill everything you ever loved and then move into the country, murdering and pillaging as they went."

That silenced some of them, but the chatter continued. Evan wasn't sure he wanted to stay behind the walls, but he touched them to reassure himself.

They were thick, made of rock many feet thick. They were strong, and difficult to climb.

Even though that monster had made it.

"We can hold them back here, and wait for reinforcements to arrive," Evan called out. "You are men of Chathem and will stand strong." Out of sheer luck, his voice didn't waver and break.

The army continued to pour out of the trees. They lined up, fierce eyes watching the defenders on the wall.

Then, out of the center, a group on horseback emerged. Evan's eyes were drawn to the man in the lead as he took his horse up to the river and splashed into the shallows.

There, horse up to its knees, he stopped.

"If you surrender now, I may let you live," the man on horseback called.

It was silent, except for the flow of the river.

Evan wondered if he was telling the truth, wondered who this man was. He didn't look particularly impressive. He wasn't large, or muscular, or even that tall.

But even from this distance he could see something in the man's eyes. A fire, a terrible ability to do whatever he needed to do for power. An unquenchable thirst for it.

And in those eyes Evan found a strange kindred.

It made him uncomfortable, it made him squirm. Was this the kind of man he would be? Willing to lead an army to take whatever he wanted by force?

He thought about surrendering, how much easier it would be. He could finally give up his titles, finally be rid of the responsibility. Evan looked up and down the line of men.

And then his eyes met Sam.

A man not even of this land, and still willing to stay and fight when he could have run. He owed no allegiance to Evan or the Hornbloods, but had sacrificed to train the others and to build this castle.

Even now, he saw Sam was tired. They all were.

From the men on the wall to the women and children inside, they wouldn't survive if the Belmarch got inside these walls, no matter if it was by surrender or force.

So Evan decided. He sheathed his sword.

"Your Highness, what are you doing?" Sam asked.

"Giving him an answer." Evan walked to the nearest archer and took the bow from him. The man gave it up, wide-eyed in surprise.

He took up an arrow, fitted it to the bow, and raised it. The feather tickled his cheek, and Evan breathed deep, remembering all his training.

He let fly the arrow, and it whistled into the air. It splashed into the river just before the horse and rider, making it shy away and whinny.

"This is Chathem land. As the sworn protector, I will give you one chance to go back. Any invasion of these lands will be met with force." Evan handed the bow back and watched the man.

He had regained control of his steed, still in the shallows. Tension crackled in the air.

"You will regret this." He turned and walked back into Belmarch, but only to talk to the other men on horseback.

Evan wanted to breathe a sigh of relief, but knew that it wouldn't be that easy.

The men scattered, kicking their horses into action and traveling up and down the bank. Orders were passed in the Belmarch tongue, and a great cry rang out from them. It billowed across the river, impossibly loud from the great army.

Evan could only watch, helpless, as the infantry waded into the river and began to cross.

25

FIRE

Sam watched the enemy advance, exchanging his spear for a bow. He wished Ned was beside him, he was so much better of a shot than he was, but as he looked down he almost chuckled.

There were more than enough targets down there. If he missed there was something wrong with him.

"Archers, ready." The high walls extended their range well into the river, but not all the way. The enemy troops splashed into the shallows where the river was the narrowest.

Just as they'd planned.

Sam joined the others, nocking an arrow to the string and pulling back.

"Fire!" Levitus yelled.

He sighted at one soldier wielding an axe above his head and let loose. A hundred arrows flew into the air, louder than a flock of birds and deadly.

The first rank was carrying ladders, hastily constructed in the forest beyond. The arrows landed, almost half on their mark, and men screamed and shouted as they dropped.

The defenders didn't have time to celebrate though, because they kept coming on, augmented by archers of their own.

"Aim for the ladder carriers," Sam shouted. The second volley wasn't as strong, nor was it as effective, and the bow firing dissolved into individual shots.

Sam ducked as a return arrow flew over his head, whistling by his ear. He went back up, aiming for the enemy who shot it, but couldn't find him. He shifted his focus to another and let loose.

Bodies started to pile up in the river, hampering the advance of the Belmarch. Splashes mixed with shouts, and the smell of death quickly started to blow over them.

He was using arrows too quickly and soon found himself down to three. "Arrows," he called, joining in the chorus that ran down the wall.

Men and young boys scrambled up the wall, bringing what they could. Dale was one of them, no archer himself, and brought Sam a bundled.

"How goes it?" he asked as Sam took them and stashed them at the base of the wall.

Sam hazarded another glance. "They're making it to our side," he said with dismay. He had hoped that they would have slowed them down more than that, but a few ladder carriers were already scrambling up the rocks.

Down the wall a man screamed and tumbled off the wall, smashing on the rocks below. His scream ended abruptly.

"Tell me you have something that will make them unwelcome," Dale said.

Sam grinned and smacked him on the shoulder. "Better get back to it."

Dale tipped his fist at him, then scrambled off, ducking down low to avoid the arrows flying overhead.

He was breathing hard now. The air smelled of blood and sweat, and sounds overwhelmed his senses.

He glanced over to the Duke. He looked untouched, and Sam was glad. The man had taken a heavy blow earlier, but he wasn't even favoring his right side.

Maybe it wasn't as bad as he thought.

An arrow clattered on the wall next to him.

Sam flinched. A few more inches to one side and it would have found his head.

He pulled back his bow and hopped up, taking aim at a ladder carrier below. His arrow found its mark, and the man crumpled to the ground, the ladder clattering back into the river.

It started to get washed away, but another group of men grabbed it. Up to the east of him ladders were going up to the wall.

"They're going to get up!" Sam pointed to them, and the Duke saw.

"Torch," he commanded. "Light them."

The order passed down the wall, and torches were lit and passed along. The first ladder hit just as they threw the torches over the side.

Sam threw his own, and counted to three. The sound of the brush and dry leaves they had placed and hid beneath the wall catching flame came a second later.

His heart pounded as he waited, hoping that it would work.

Then, another monster was there, on the wall.

Sam jumped up, grabbed at his spear as it killed a soldier near him.

Another was able to cut at it, but then it turned on him. It moved like lightning, it was so fast.

But it was distracted and had its back to him. Sam thrust with the spear, catching it just below the nape of the neck.

He pushed with all his might, and it went through reluctantly. The thing went limp, taking his spear with it.

Sam scrambled to grab at it, was just able to pull it free before the body tumbled into the courtyard.

Behind, Trent stood wide eyed. "Thank you."

"Back to the wall," Sam said, wiping the blood off his face. Was it the monster's or his own?

His body felt fine.

The base of the wall was glowing, smoke coming up like a curtain. The ladders they were using had gotten wet on the trip over, but they were smoking now.

And the base of them were on fire.

Sam kicked one over, pushing it back with the butt of his spear, and it toppled backward. "Brush, bring up the brush."

He tossed one bundle they had staged up on the wall, a mixture of brush and shavings from the workshop.

They caught fire quickly, adding to the conflagration below, and it drove the Belmarch back. More bundles of them came up from below, and the defenders started being more selective with their targets.

Bowstring still twanged, and arrow still flew, but they were targeted at the enemy archers, who were starting to trickle down as the flames pushed them back.

Sam watched them, just peeking over the edge of the wall. With the Golden River to the east and the northern wall aflame, they only had one real choice.

Trumpets sounded again. Men burst from the trees carrying a large log by the cut down branches. The front had been sharpened to a tip and they had makeshift shields above their heads.

They splashed into the river, but headed west, downstream.

Just as we thought. Sam added another bundle to the fire below, taking pleasure as it whooshed into flames.

The leader was smart, and he understood the castle's weakness. While they tried to keep the ladders from the wall the battering ram crossed behind the attackers.

They were headed for the gate.

They were doing it. Evan looked out over the wall and watched them going for the gate.

Behind the battering ram streamed the rest of the army.

There were so many. Too many to count. Evan felt the rock in the pit of his stomach grow harder and harder.

How are we going to survive?

They were less than two hundred, and thousands were crossing. All they had were bows and a few small arms, but they had the arms of thousands.

Evan swallowed but ducked back behind the wall to think. Up and down the wall men were still fighting, firing arrows or pushing off the remaining ladders, or throwing more bundles over the wall to add to the fire burning beneath them.

It was too much. Evan closed his eyes, let the shouts and screams and sounds of the fire and death fade away.

He was back with Yand, looking over the low hill, the first moment he had seen the castle. It was smaller than he expected, but even from the distance the walls seemed big and solid. Men streamed over the construction, working to raise the fortress up out of the earth from where it slept.

It was always a fool's errand, to build so close to the Belmarch and their warlike ways, but it was not his position to question, only to obey.

His father had taught him that lesson, or tried to. Over and over he resisted, and now Evan knew why.

For one day, after he had taken his proper place, he would lead the Hornblood lands in his father's stead.

Evan's eyes snapped open, and he sucked in a deep breath. It had all been for this reason, all the years of disobedience, the nights in the taverns, the misbehavior when he knew it would embarrass his family.

The curse that he had brought about himself would cause the downfall of his house and all the people he cared about.

But it wasn't going to happen in the future, it was happening now. Even as he looked, men were dying. An arrow took a man to his left in the neck, and he crumpled up against the wall clutching at it until his blood was drained and his life over.

Haml, a young mason. Barely twenty summers old, and a long life ahead of him.

His blank, lifeless eyes stared up at Evan, who scrambled back to try and escape that accusing gaze.

It was his fault. He touched what was forbidden, he brought this down upon them.

And now there was no way out. The gate was barred, a long line of enemies behind it ready to rush in.

They would destroy it.

They would make it inside.

They would kill him and everyone else, and then they would sweep south, spoiling the land and desecrating his home.

Blood would well up from the ground, and the last of their people would either flee or be enslaved.

Evan hung his head in shame. He had brought this on them.

"Duke Hornblood." Someone grabbed his arm. "They are at the gate now. You need to give the order."

"Order?" Evan was in a daze. He could barely think. There was no use in trying, they would still kill them all.

Sam knelt down in front of him, eye to eye. "You are a Duke of Hornblood. Look at these men."

He followed Sam's finger. To the west men were still fighting, firing arrow after arrow with grim looks on their faces.

One of them had a bandage wrapped around his left eye, but he still fought on. Another was handing arrows out, cradling an arm smashed to bits.

"You don't understand, I'm cursed."

"That's enough out of you. On your feet like a man." Sam pulled him up.

Evan stared at him, shocked at how he spoke.

"You can either die here as a sniveling coward, too afraid to lead your men, or you can choose a different path."

Anger, anger at the words brought him back to his sense. The way he insulted him, a Duke of Hornblood, how little he knew him.

"What will it be, Your Highness?" Sam spit the word out like it was a foul taste. "A cursed coward, or a true leader?"

There were men here, men that deserved to live. He didn't deserve anything, not to be a Duke or the future Archduke, nor had he earned their respect.

And yet, they still gave it. They could have killed him long ago, but they chose to listen to him.

Like the men in those stories his mother had given him.

"I can't let them down." Sam smiled as Evan spoke. "Are we destined to the path that was laid before us?" Evan asked.

Sam wavered, looked away. Even though the fire beneath the wall cast an orange glow on him, his face fell into shadow.

"I can only hope that a man can change." Evan sensed more desire in Sam, a desire to say something else, something deeper, but it came and went.

I'm not the only one fighting a destiny.

"Then, if we can change, let us change together." Evan held out a hand. Sam looked up, then took it. "Tonight is the last night I ever pitied myself. Tonight is the last night I didn't think of myself of a Duke of Hornblood."

He looked back out over the raging river of men passing through the river. "This may be my last night alive. I don't want to live with any regrets."

"Nor do I," Sam said. Evan realized the kinship that lay between them, a man so easy to talk with him as an equal.

"Then I would ask a former prince and knight to fight with me, by my side," Evan said. Sam's eyes opened wide in shock. "Whatever man you used to be, whatever the reasons you left that life, we need you for who you are, not for who you were."

"I was never a prince," Sam said, eyes glistening in the firelight. "But I hated the killing. It seemed so senseless."

"If we don't stop them, there will be more killing. Surely, you can see that?"

A boom sounded at the gate. Sam turned to it. Another one followed, and then they were coming at a steady pace.

Evan clasped his shoulder. Sam nodded. Evan rose his voice and shouted, "To the gate!"

26

WELCOMING PARTY

The group of men waiting in the courtyard sprang up and sprinted to the southern wall. Another band rose from their hiding positions on the east wall and started firing arrows into the attackers.

Evan nodded to Sam, then ducked down and sprinted to the gatehouse. He passed by men doing their best, and he gave them what little encouragement he could, all the while knowing it wouldn't be enough.

But in every eye he saw there was a hardened resilience, a desire to fight ingrained deep within. No one doubted the fight would be difficult, but they knew that it could be done.

A random stone on the battlements tripped him, and Evan almost stumbled over the side, but at the last minute he caught himself, slamming into the hard rock. His right shoulder screamed in a pain that flared and traveled down his arm, but he picked himself up, brushed off his scraped hands, and kept going.

The Belmarch were not going to let up with a little bit of archery and were returning fire where they could. The fires along the north side helped, blinding them, and most of their arrows went high or low, clattering harmlessly.

But not every one.

A man twirled in front of him, clutching at an arrow sprouting from his shoulder. Evan caught him and laid him against the wall, wishing someone else would come to help. None did. His breathing was labored as Evan propped him up and told him to get ready.

"This will hurt." Evan grasped the rough arrow shaft, and the man closed his eyes with a grimace. With a quick motion, one he had only seen once but read about, Evan snapped the shaft of the arrow. Blood spurted from the shaft, and Evan held his hand against it.

The wounded man groaned, and clamped down with gritted teeth, but Evan couldn't stay with him. He called another soldier over. "Put a bandage on that and make sure the bleeding stops."

Evan made sure one more time that he was taken care of, then kept going.

The percussive sounds of the battering ram had changed. It was no longer a thick, hollow sound, but there were tiny hints of splinters. Smoke rose from the gatehouse, a good sign, and Evan took a peek over the side before he went in.

Soldiers were lined up below, makeshift shields of wood and mud held above them. One archer spied him and sent an arrow his way, so Evan ducked back behind the wall and into the gatehouse.

The smoke from the fire made his eyes water, and he crouched down to avoid being overwhelmed by the smell. "Is it ready?"

"Yes, Your Highness," Levitus said, waiting by the pot stirred by a younger mason.

"Good, do it now." Each boom made him wince, the sound getting hollower and hollower. It took three men to pick up the pot and carry it to the hole, a great cloud of steam rising off it as they did.

An arrow found its way up the murder hole, almost making them jump back, but momentum carried them on. They tipped and a great gush of a waterfall came out, leaking steam that mingled with the dark black smoke already hovering at the roof.

Men screamed below, scalded by the hot water, and ran out. The booms stopped for a blessed moment, but Evan knew that soon they would return.

But, in the meantime, the Belmarch were stopped and exposed. Other men brought in chunks of rock, cut from the masons to be as jagged as they could get them.

Evan took up one too, almost cutting himself on a sharp edge. One by one they lined up to toss them below, another delaying tactic.

But what are we delaying them until? Evan was next, and he threw down the rock before sliding out of the way.

The water and rock were having their intended effect though, and the battering ram lay abandoned on the ground. Evan could see it through a corner of one of the murder holes.

It moved as more Belmarch soldiers tried to pick it up, but another pot of water was already boiling and was added to discourage them.

Now the smell of blood mixed with smoke and water, and it was starting to make him sick. Evan gave them some encouragement but went back through the gatehouse door to get some fresh air and see how the rest of the defenders were faring.

They were putting up a fight and wearing the Belmarch down. More rocks were being thrown outside, since they was easier to access.

Evan stole between merlons until he was next to Levitus. "How bad are the losses?"

Levitus fired off an arrow, grim-faced as there was a scream off in the distance. "Not as bad as I expected, worse than I hoped. Keeping them off the wall with that fire was a neat trick, but I'm not sure it will last that long."

Evan looked to the northern wall, where he had assigned Sam to. "Every second counts." He glanced into the sky, a great cloud of smoke filling it and drifting, obscuring the stars.

The night had brought a chill, one he hadn't felt while he was moving, but now made him shiver as it dried his sweat. *What am I waiting for? Help from my father?*

"We could use some reinforcements, if you were planning on a miracle," Levitus said.

Evan snorted. "If I could produce it, I would have already." He snuck a glance over the wall. The steady stream of soldiers had lightened, and there were no archers in the immediate vicinity.

With the momentary lull, Evan was able to get his first good look at the Belmarch army. That they were fighters, he had no doubt.

Every one was clad in fighting leathers, and every one had a weapon of iron. Most were simple swords, curved but wicked looking, but there were a few spears thrown in for good measure.

They crossed the stream even as he watched, forming a cluster at the trees to the west. He had a glimmer of hope as he watched them mull about, trying to keep out of arrow range.

They might be able to make it after all. The thought caught in his throat, made him almost breathless.

Then, the steady pounding of the battering ram began again.

27

THE BEACON

The fires were dying down on the north wall. They still sent up great plumes of thick, black smoke, but the heat Sam once felt from them was getting less and less.

Despite their attempts to keep it going, they were running out of the tinder and wood shaving bundles they had made and had burned through all of the fuel they had placed there beforehand.

And the rate of fire they were taking from the Belmarch was getting worse. Sam took a peek, then ducked his head back as three arrows clattered around him. The ladders were back too, smacking against the wall even though the fires still raged.

"They're wetting them," Trent said as he fired off another arrow. "It's protecting the ladders from the fires."

Sam grimaced. He hadn't planned on them finding a way of protecting the ladders, and cursed himself for not thinking of how easy it would be to wet them sooner. Despite it, they were falling into his trap.

"Start bringing the men in, two at a time, from the outer edges. Pass the word, we need to fall back."

"Already?" Trent asked.

Sam jerked his head to the wall and popped up to get another shot off. An arrow flew by his cheek, but he was able to aim at an attacker in the river.

He never knew if he hit the man or not, though, because he had to fall back down under cover as soon as he could. *There are too many of them.*

Trent was wide eyed. "I'll pass the word."

He turned and did it as quietly as he could. They had a plan, but Sam wondered when it would fall apart.

The sounds of battle helped hide the word being passed, and since they were taking so much fire, it felt more natural to have fewer men. Their absence would be felt less, and Sam knew the only way this would work is if they had the element of surprise.

At the end of it, however, he wasn't sure what they would do.

A ladder fell onto the wall in front of him, spraying him with ice cold droplets of water. Sam jumped back in surprise, then readied to push it over with his spear, but a man was almost at the top.

Or what used to be a man.

Sam had to choke down his fear, despite seeing them before, and pushed with all his weight against the ladder, but the monster grabbed onto the shaft before he could do so, and wrenched.

The spear flew out of his hand, and his shoulder and arm almost came with it. His heart leaped into his throat as Sam pulled his backup sword like lightning.

The monster was up and over the wall before he could finish, its own blade singing a deadly song as it struck at Sam's throat.

He dropped, twisting and sliding his blade across the monster's abdomen, bringing a spray of blood as it cut below its meager armor.

Sam didn't even have time to shout for help before it was at him again, sword flashing so fast it was a blur.

He tried to keep up, backing away as he parried, the monster snarling at him. Froth dripped from its fangs, breath worse than a rotten carcass.

Sam lost ground, until Trent flew in with a thrust from over his shoulder and a deafening battle cry. Cut all over, Sam still turned to help, pressing the attack.

At first, they struggled to get in sync, so much so that the monster rigged a gash down Trent's leg.

When his blade whistled by Sam's throat, his mind cleared. The vision of him being a few inches closer was all he needed.

"Left," Sam said, lunging to the right. Trent, barely a hair behind him, cut from the left.

The monster parried Trent, but couldn't get to Sam in time, and leaped back with a hole in its leg.

They moved together, Sam not needing to say anything. He could sense Trent out of the corner of his eye.

Perfectly in sync, they became a whirlwind of death. Cuts bloomed on the monster, who could barely keep from a mortal wound, backing up one step at a time.

Behind it, another ladder had appeared on the wall, with Belmarch soldiers pouring over it. Someone behind him was yelling for a retreat, almost distracting Sam.

But he remembered all those who were locked away in the Keep, safe for now from the murderous hands of their enemies.

The women, the children. Belinda and her child. Joseph. *Martha*.

He couldn't lose, not now. With one last battle cry Sam sprung forward, rolling underneath the monster's grasp, and hamstringing it.

Seconds later, its head fell to the floor, rapidly changing back to that of a man, helped by a dripping blade in Trent's hand.

Sam gasped for breath, the adrenaline pulling back long enough to let him realize what kind of situation they were in.

Men were retreating, running back down the stairs, as the Belmarch gained more and more of a foothold on the battlements. A group of five or six were coming for them now.

"Sam," Trent warned.

"Go." He scooped up his bow and turned. He followed Trent to the stairs as more and more ladders sprung up.

They were ahead of them now, but Sam couldn't stop now. They attacked, setting the attackers on their heels.

They were savage fighters, inflicting more wounds on the two defenders who by this time were the last on the wall, but Sam and Trent had the upper hand in skill, and overwhelmed them.

With a few new wounds, they made it to the stairs. Pain was catching up to Sam now, the ache of battle and the fatigue of swinging his sword setting in.

But, one foot in front of another, he descended the stairs to the courtyard, until soft earth was once again beneath his feet.

He took one glance behind him. Belmarch attackers were streaming over the walls and following them into the courtyard.

A hundred feet away, the defender's ladder up the wall shone like a beacon, the only way to safety now.

Sam gritted his teeth and ran through the pain.

28

UNRAVELING PLANS

Blood streamed down Evan's head, warm and sticky. His hand went to the wound, expecting the worst. No arrow, nothing lodged in his skull.

Only a flesh wound. He breathed a sigh of relief and returned the favor, catching an enemy archer in the eye.

"There are too many," Levitus said. "We need to fall back."

"No, it's too soon."

The dread in the pit of his stomach still hadn't gone away. They had a plan to fall back to the Keep, but afterward...

And now, it was coming faster than he wanted. Mathew ran up to them, ducking for cover as he went. "We've lost the northern wall and are retreating from the west."

Evan whirled, dismayed to see the northern wall almost completely filled with Belmarchers. Not a single defender was left on the wall, at least not any that were still alive. A few bodies were visible between the legs of the attackers.

More dead. *How many more need to die?* Evan wanted to sit down, to go back to his home, to be done with this.

But here were two men right beside him who needed him, eyes boring into his soul.

And the men on the west wall were retreating back to them, eyes on the attackers as they rounded the corner.

They could put up a fight for a few more minutes, but not much longer, and the multitude outside the gates was growing.

"Give them one last bath, then we'll go." Evan reached down deep, trying to tell if it was the right decision, but there was only silence and the deep well of self-doubt.

But he was a Hornblood, a branch of the family that kept the Hornwood alive and thriving. Protector of the Everlong.

He tried to run through the old sayings, hoping that they would make him feel better.

Somehow, they did. He remembered his ancestors, and the men in the stories, how they overcame monsters and storms, traveled across seas and came out of deserts to triumph on the other side.

"One more, yes, Your Highness." Mathew was wearing a big grin, and sprinted back inside the gatehouse.

"Start getting them into the walls, let have them attack, and pull up the ladder. We don't want any unwelcome visitors," Evan said.

Levitus saluted and disappeared, running to the west and shouting as he did. His voice was enveloped in the din and clash of the fighting.

They were making an orderly escape, and holding their own against the Belmarch, on the west wall. Evan drew his sword and advanced across the battlements, smelling the ash and smoke of the fire and urging it on.

It took him no time to round the corner, passing a stream of men who glanced at him with exhausted faces covered in blood and ash.

He could taste it in the air, bitter and sour, and wished again for the clear air of peace.

Then, he was in the thick of fighting and advanced through the wavering line.

"Fall back," Evan ordered, even as he pushed through to attack. He struck out, catching a Belmarcher in the gut, whose eyes widened in shock as he clutched at his belly.

Evan kicked him back, using his body to knock over another few attackers, and slipped into the forms.

His mind went blank, and all he could see were the weapons and movements of the men he fought.

Swords flashed at him, but he parried them or dodged, and struck back with lightning speed.

He felt no exhaustion, felt no weight, but let himself go. *This is what Yand was trying to teach me.* The thought floated in his mind, like he was looking down on his body.

They could only come at him two at a time, and he used it to his advantage. Bodies started to pile up as he killed one after the other.

The attackers were bogged down and had to climb over the dead bodies of their friends and countrymen to reach him, and Evan kept up the fight, making them pay dearly.

His lungs burned, his heart pounded, but the forms came like water.

Strike after strike, blow after blow, he flowed. Evan was aware that he was getting hit, but nothing was serious enough for him to stop.

Then, one last man charged, swinging an axe down from over his head.

Evan sidestepped, clipped him with his foot, and pushed him over the edge of the wall and back to the outside.

His scream was cut short a second later.

The Belmarch stared at him, stopped on the wall.

Exhaustion caught up to him like a wave, smashing into his body, and he almost crumpled over, but still they just looked at him.

Someone was yelling his name. He looked back for just a second. It was Levitus calling him.

Evan realized he alone was left standing on the west wall.

The Belmarch backed up, looking for the nearest stairs, and none would go forward.

Evan saw they were trying to cut him off and turned and ran back.

His feet slapped against the hard stone, legs protesting and screaming, as Levitus waved him over to the trapdoor.

The ladder they had put into the courtyard side of the newest walls leading to the Keep was gone.

But there were men at the stairs, barely a few feet in front of him, and Belmarch archers were shooting at him.

Evan wasn't sure he was going to make it before they would, and tried to increase his pace, but his legs felt like stone.

He was only a few feet away when a Belmarcher jumped up on the wall, blocking his path, and turned to face him with sword and shield at the ready.

It was too late. He wasn't going to make it.

29

AN OPPORTUNE TIME

A sword blossomed from the Belmarcher's throat, and he slipped to his knees.

Sam pulled his sword free of the man and kicked the body back down the wall.

Evan staggered the last few feet, taking Sam's hand, and he was almost pulled down the trapdoor ladder.

It slammed shut with a bang, and Sam slid the locking bar in place.

"Glad you made it," Sam said as pounding started on the trapdoor. "It might not take them long to get through it, even though it's four inch thick oak."

Evan recovered his breath. "How many made it?"

"I'm not sure." Men were lining the hollow wall, shooting arrows into the courtyard attackers. They had nowhere to go and were trying to stay out of range.

Evan peered out an arrow hole. Belmarchers were clustered up at the entrance to the stairs, and all along it.

Their numbers were working against them now, just like Sam had said.

Evan leaned his head against the cold stone and took a moment to recover. His body was beaten, and he hadn't realized how badly his right shoulder hurt.

As he stood it lanced with pain, and he involuntarily cried out.

"Your Highness!" Sam was by his side.

"Just my shoulder. How much time do you think we have?"

Sam watched him warily, examining him for major injuries, then glanced at the trapdoor. "An hour, at most. Probably less."

"Well then, let's give them something to think about." Evan smiled but knew that he couldn't pull a bow back now. Not with this pain.

He also had a big gash near his knee, but it had clotted over and wasn't bleeding, so he put weight on his leg.

It didn't hurt that badly, and he could walk well enough. Evan walked down the small corridor, pausing as defenders drew back their bows to shoot.

The supply of arrows was low. Dangerously low, and they had only the reserve in the Keep left.

"Make them count," Evan said. He watched an older mason sight, breathe deep, and loose.

Outside, he was rewarded by a shout of pain.

The Belmarch were trying to shoot back, but the arrowslits were doing their job well. Nothing was getting through.

The pounding started back, and Evan turned to the gate. He hadn't realized it had stopped.

One final parting gift. He hoped it had killed as many as possible.

Evan was at a loss for what to do now. He couldn't fight back, not now, and he couldn't stop them from coming in the gate.

They were going to breach it soon, if they didn't find a way into their hastily constructed tunnels, and there was nothing he could do but listen to the mayhem and shouting around him and smell the blood and excrement of battle.

Then, the gate gave way. He winced at the sound of the crunch, then splintering, and the great cheer from the Belmarch outside.

Thousands of them raised their voices in victory, the blood lust thick.

Evan glanced down at his blade. It was dripping blood into the dust. He swung it, trying to get most of it off, and stalked back toward the entrance.

Through the arrowslit, he saw the Belmarch ripping back the remains of the gate and portcullis.

They were eager and overcome with the heat of the battle.

"Divide, half take the left, the other focus on the right," Evan ordered. His command was passed down the tunnel. "They are coming."

Then, the gate was breached, and Belmarch climbed in between the walls.

They were confused to find no one there, until the arrows started.

The first attackers died quickly, but more took their place. They stepped over the bodies of their comrades and rushed forward.

Some stopped, trying to slide spears and swords through the arrowslits.

Evan rewarded one of them with a sword to the throat. He fell back with a bubbling gurgle and back into the dust.

It was the most Evan could do. He felt powerless now, as the Belmarch advanced in the courtyard and through the gate.

"We don't have enough room to avoid them," Evan shouted, jumping back as a sword poked at him.

He trapped it with his foot, then slashed at the attacker holding onto it.

"I was hoping we could hold out longer," Sam said, grimly firing arrows out towards the men in the courtyard. He picked up his last one. "It might be time to get back into the Keep."

Evan didn't want to give the order. A man down the tunnel screamed, his voice echoing severely, and slumped to the ground, a spear in him.

He couldn't see the sky, but it was dark even with the torches lining the tunnel.

"Fall back to the Keep." The flow of arrows had trickled to a stream, and the Belmarch in the courtyard were advancing to the wall without fear.

The words were bitter in his mouth, like he had failed once again. Only this time instead of him waking up in the gutter they would all be dead.

Every one of them.

Men shuffled back, a few of them wounded enough to be pulled, and the tunnel emptied into the Keep.

"Sam, you first." Evan pointed down the tunnel.

Sam nodded, then followed the others.

Evan took one last look, then joined him.

The Keep was filled, men standing at the entrance door that had been blocked and reinforced. Even though it was going to be a struggle, Evan knew that their enemy would get the battering ram through.

"Is everything ready?" Torchlight flickered over the group of them. Bill had been leading the group in the other tunnel, and he stepped forward now into the orange glow.

"It is ready. At your command."

Evan glanced at the two open doors. If they waited too long...

But they couldn't do it too early. The Belmarch were at the door, pounding on it in vain.

They shouted back for the battering ram.

Men shifted in the hallway, an uncomfortable silence taking over.

The Belmarch stopped pounding, and Evan stood and watched the door, his entire world narrowing to it.

"Not yet," he whispered, dry mouth cracking.

30

THE RED DAY

Men stood in the quiet of the night, breathing heavily. The torches flickered and consumed their fuel, shedding a small amount of heat on the wounded and broken gathered there.

Evan felt himself pulled into a sense of peace, even though they could hear the scraping and shouting of the Belmarch attackers.

Three ways in, and soon it would be none. Evan licked his lips, tasting sweat, blood, and ash all mixed together.

He thought he should say something, and gathered his words. His father would know what words were needed.

But I'm not my father. He was his own man, and in this moment he had to act like it.

"No matter what happens," he hated how final the words came out, but pressed on, "I can die well knowing we did our best."

"The night is not yet over," Sam said, stepping out of the shadows. He was covered in cuts, and his left eye was swollen shut. He looked like walking death. "We have hope yet."

"Hope for the morning, hope for a new day," Evan said. The gloom of the night was indeed lifting, the blackness he thought would go on forever turning to a light gray as the light of morning twilight streamed in.

"A better life," Bill said.

"And time with those we hold most dear," Sam whispered. The tone in the hallway had changed.

Inside Evan, the fear melted away. He wiped off his sword and sheathed it, straightened his back, and turned back to the door.

"Let them come and meet the men of Chathem."

He waited, with all the others, as the Belmarch shuffled the battering ram in through the broken gate and down between the walls they were trapped between.

Men still beat at the trapdoors, but had not gotten through.

Feet tramped close, then orders were called, and with a great shout they came.

Boom.

The first blow echoed through the hall. Dust shifted and fell from up above. Evan felt it through his feet.

"Hold." Men were pressed up against him, waiting in anticipation thick like a morning fog upon the river.

They brought the ram back, then rushed forward again.

Boom.

The braces held, the door shivered.

They went back again.

Boom.

Evan looked to Sam, who nodded. "Take them down."

Bill slipped into the east tunnel, Sam the west, carrying their large, wooden mallets.

Evan watched the door.

Boom.

It had given more than the last time. The wood wouldn't hold up forever.

Boom.

Now there was another sound, a knocking hollow sound, drifting through each door.

The Belmarch didn't seem to notice, but the energy in the hall heightened.

Evan held his breath.

Bill reappeared, rushed through the door, and slammed it. Sam followed a few seconds later.

Boom.

Evan frowned, his entire face tightening. He glanced at Sam. "I thought it was supposed to fall right away."

Sam's lips tightened. "The other beams might be holding tighter than I anticipated."

"Your Highness, they might be at the walls," Levitus said. "We should take the men up." His left arm hung at his side, unnaturally limp.

"Sam, make this work," Evan said, grasping his arm. To the others, "To your stations."

He turned and led his third of the men up the stairs to the right.

Sam didn't know why it wasn't working. They had notched the beams right, the masons had put in the wall the way he had asked.

But nothing happened.

Boom.

The sound rattled his skull. The walls were still standing. They shouldn't be.

Boom.

Sam realized what had happened, and then the weight of how to fix it fell upon him.

Bill was still here, and Trent. "The walls need to be pushed."

"Pushed?" Bill asked, eyebrows drawn down.

He thought it could be just one. "Lock the door behind me if I don't make it."

Sam strode through the door.

"Sam, no," Trent said, trying to hold him back. *He was a smart man.*

"I'll just start it, I'll be back through before you know it."

"You might not make it, you might..." There was a real fear in Trent's eyes.

"I know." Emotion choked at his throat. "Take care... I am proud of you."

He broke away from Trent's grasp and was in the tunnel of walls a second later. Sam collected himself, looked up at the wall, and put his hands against them.

The stone, rough and jagged beneath his hands, was cold. *Boom.*

He couldn't wait any longer.0020Sam dug his feet into the dirt, squatted, and pushed.

It was too big, too heavy.

Try as he might, Sam could not budge it. He strained, he struggled.

Then, two more pairs of hands joined his, Bill on his right and Trent on his left.

"No, go back," he gasped.

"You need the help," Bill said.

"I'm not leaving you," Trent said.

Feeling a mixture of relief and sadness, Sam bore down and pushed again, his feet digging into the earth.

The wall budged.

Evan was the first onto the wall, the sky a light gray and a fresh breeze blowing from the south.

The sight made his heart drop. Belmarch filled the court-yard, were assembled all along the outside of the southern wall.

And the battering ram was ready for another hit.

"Aim for those on the ram," Evan said. The twenty or so men who could still shoot arrows fired.

He put his hands on the edge of the wall, watching the clouds up above turn orange. There was no escape, there was no way out.

And the Belmarch still came, down to a trickle of horses and carts, across the river.

They were invading.

The man on the horse had taken up position with the rest of his leadership on the plain outside the walls.

Evan could feel his eyes on him, and the victory he must be pleased about.

They even had reinforcements coming up, a great army emerging from the forest to the southwest.

All seemed lost.

Still, he was at peace. They still had to get in the Keep, and it would cost them dearly, maybe enough to slow them down enough so that the others could flee.

He turned his attention to the walls, watching them closely. Nothing happened.

Men were setting fire to the trapdoors now, trying to weaken them enough to get in.

"Come on," Evan whispered. The defenders peppered them with arrows, but there were too many to make much of a difference.

Belmarch invaders surrounded the newly built walls. He couldn't ask for a better time.

Then, the left wall leaned in. Evan leaned in looking closer.

It teetered, then started to topple.

Just like Sam had said, the walls collapsed, first the right side, then the left.

The Keep rumbled, the sound like rolling thunder. Men screamed and were silenced, great clouds of dust rose.

Evan felt the tremor through the stone and struggled to stay on his feet.

He coughed, trying to keep the dust out of his lungs, and the others on the wall fell back.

When it cleared, the courtyard was chaos. None of the Belmarch in between the walls had survived, and now stone blocked the entrance.

A good portion of those on the other side hadn't been able to escape either, and the attackers were in a state of total confusion.

"It worked," Evan whispered. Horns sounded, but they were not the horns of the Belmarch.

They were the horns of Hornblood.

Evan looked to the south, where the sound had come from.

The army was charging, but they weren't from Belmarch.

It was the King of Chathem, the banner of his own father flying by his side.

Already confused, the Belmarch were unprepared for the attack on their flank. The man on horseback struggled to form up ranks, but it was too late.

Evan watched as the Chathem army slammed into the Belmarch, ripping them in two, and pushing them to the Black River.

He sank to his knees, overwhelmed at the turn of events. His death was no longer inevitable.

Evan Hornblood looked to the light of the morning sky and felt peace wash over him like warmth.

Epilogue

Evan felt his legs shake as he walked down the stairs to the entrance of the Keep, the feeling and sounds bouncing around inside those of joy and exuberance.

Word had spread of the King's arrival, and women and children rushed past him to see.

At the entrance the left most door was open, blocked with rubble.

Sam, Trent, and Bill were inside being seen to by Martha and a few others. They were bruised and beaten, black and blue on anything that was visible, and Sam's left leg was broken.

"It worked." Evan knelt down next to Sam, clasping his hand. "They're routing the Belmarch, who are fleeing back to their own land. I hope that they will stay there."

"I hope for peace," Sam said.

"Excuse me, Your Highness," Martha said. Evan rose, gave her his place, and sat to rest.

His body ached, and his shoulder shot pain down his arm anytime he moved it.

But they had made it. They had survived the attack.

And he had held. He had been a man of Hornblood.

When they were finally able to clear the rubble enough to get outside it was after noon.

Evan was the first to greet the King, who strode into the Keep with flashing eyes and teeth. Evan's father, the Archduke of Hornblood, was at his side, still bandaged from his previous wounds, and Rhys was smiling behind them.

Evan couldn't believe his eyes, but Rhys just motioned to him and kept smiling.

The King commended Evan on his work holding until they could arrive, making mention of being held up by eastern raiders.

"It was not me, Your Honor," Evan said. "These men fought bravely, valiantly, and built well. They are the ones who should be commended."

"Well noted." The King waved to an adviser and whispered in his ear.

The Archduke pulled him to the side and asked for a word in private. Evan nodded and led him to his study, catching Rhys by the arm before he went.

"Was this your doing?"

"It's a long story, I'll tell you about it another time," Rhys said, "but I still have friends in Ironwood."

In Evan's study, his father looked first upon the crest on the wall, a slight smile on his lips. "You have done... more than I ever thought of you, my son."

"I wasn't ready to take your place," Evan said, startling him. "And I spent so long trying to run from it. I never really knew that was what I was doing all these years."

The Archduke studied him, his face turning tender for what seemed to Evan to be the first time.

"I know. You will be ready, when the time comes." The Archduke smiled and embraced his son.

Sam and Martha wed the next week, and the defenders took a well-deserved feast to mark its occasion. Belinda stood by Martha's side, baby in hand, and although he could still see grief in her eyes, the hate was gone.

The King and his army returned to the south, leaving a hefty garrison and promise of provision.

The workers returned to work on the castle, and additional workers were sent to bolster their efforts.

Bill remained master mason and grew into the role.

Kerien became the master carpenter as Sam was occupied with his work as Overseer. No replacement was offered to Sam, and he settled into the work.

Two years later Sam stood on the Keep, repairs to the gate and wall complete, as Bill set the final stone.

He pulled Martha close in a hug as the cheer rang out around them.

The castle was complete. He looked on it with satisfaction, and the knowledge that something of him, and everyone who worked to build it, would remain with it while the walls stood.

ECLECTIC STORIES

Thank you for spending your precious time reading this book.

If stories make you salivate, learn more about lore, take an exclusive sneak peek behind the scenes, and get writing updates in my newsletter, Eric's Eclectic Stories.

As a bonus you'll get *Stories from the Deep*, a Patmos Sea Fantasy Adventure anthology that gives a glimpses of lore, extra prologues and epilogues, and character backstories.

If you aren't satisfied, unsubscribe at any time.

Join at erickercher.com.

-Eric Kercher

ALSO BY ERIC KERCHER

Patmos Sea Fantasy Adventure Series

*Fathomless Pursuit - Architect's Prize - Ironbound Path
Sunken Prey – Unanswered Prophecy – Hardened Pilgrim –
Final Peace*

Seventh Hall Chronicles

Seventh Hall - Ode to the Survivors - Bastion of the Deep

Epic of Hornblood Castle

*Siege of the Unfinished Keep – Winter at Hornblood – Branch
of the Everlong*

Castlebound Adventures

Rats in the Cellar!- Save the Cat!

Collections

Red Eagle Anthology | Searchlight Anthology

Stand Alone

Planet Reaping | Dukedom Rumble | Savage Space Salvage

ABOUT AUTHOR

Eric Kercher was born and raised in a small town on the Great Plains on good books. After attending a small state school on the east coast he joined the US Navy to serve his country and explore the world. He worked on submarines, and the world beneath the waves captivated him with all its mysteries and wonders. After spending time in larger cities, he's settled down in a quiet town with his wife and children. When not on an adventure in a good book the author enjoys creating dust woodworking, architecture, and spending time with loved ones.

Find out more at www.erickercher.com.

www.ingramcontent.com/pod-product-compliance
Lightning Source LLC
Chambersburg PA
CBHW031557310726
48974CB00003B/709